Seven Gifts
in
The Rain

Eric Hoffer Award 2019: *Winner* -- E-book fiction
Finalist -- Most thought-provoking book
Shortlist -- The Grand Prize.

The BookLife Prize: *"This is a wonderful current-day twist on fairy tales, faith, subjective morality, and the search for universal truths."*

US Review of Books: *"Perhaps the most unusual book you'll ever read, as educational and inspiring as Kahlil Gibran's* The Prophet, *but far more readable."*

"Beautifully written tales that capture the mind, heart and spirit." **-- Szoch**

"I thought this little book was charming. I much preferred it to The Shack." **-- Self Publishing Review**

"Brilliant, wise and funny book . . lingers in your head like a piece of music." **-- The Nelson Mail**

"Brilliant . . bizarre . . the details of seamanship are surreal." **-- Jenny from England**

".. beautifully written, in wonderful, simple yet perfect prose; every sentence is an individual work of art, The Sailor applying language in broad, consistently creative swathes - this is the fiction that, as writer, you wish you could write." **--Matt McAvoy**

"A beautifully conceived philosophical work"

Seven Gifts were sown deep in our world;

then the rains came . . .

"A most unusual and beautiful story."

theSailor

I would like to think this story
belongs to us all.

The copyright, however, is mine;
I wrote it.

© theSailor
5th Edition - New Year 2020
Publisher: Strange Land

See all my writings at

http://thesailor.nz

This story is not true
- as far as I know -
but I hope it holds some truths.
Unfetter your mind before reading,
as it may not be quite
what you are expecting.

The story is for Tammy
who my daughter thinks
would have understood

The Seven Gifts

Custer's Last Band

7 days in the Death of Nellie Matilda

Charlie's Angel

The Flight of a Honeybee

The Philosopher's Stone

George and the Weed

The Beauty of the Beast

The Angel Tales

Country Garden

The Journey

Gone Fishing

Leaning on a Gate

Get Thee Behind Me

The Neverending Story

I Come Not to Bring Peace

"Little children,
keep yourselves from idols"

Before the Story

BEFORE THIS STORY began there came into the world a little girl, to whom everything was possible and all things had meaning.

It was obvious to the little girl - long before it was to the scientists - that if she could imagine something then it must exist. Her mind was a part of the Universe, so anything in her mind was also, de facto, part of the Universe, and therefore, in some form, existed.

Thus her world was full of wonder and magic; peopled by daring and handsome Princes who rescued damsels in distress, saved woodcutters and milkmaids from tyranny, and rode fine white chargers across the land, their goodness proudly emblazoned across their hearts.

Before the Story

Good fought with Evil all through the early years of her life, and Good always triumphed. And so life for a little girl was simple, and she instinctively understood what was meant by the words: "Except ye be converted, and become as little children, ye shall not enter into the Kingdom of Heaven."

But her elders had no more idea of the real truth behind those words than they had of the theme that is threaded through this story. They translated words according to the dictionary; then smiled at the smug illusion of their maturity. Life was considerably more complex than any little girl could imagine, what with stock exchanges and mortgages, pension funds and life assurance, technology, social mores and atom bombs.

It was the bounden duty of adults to make little girls grow up and face the true facts of modern, civilised life. And that, undaunted by dreams, was what they did.

So the little girl was coerced out of childhood; and she carefully put away all her childish things, according to the example set her.

She laid aside her childish charm and wonder, and drew on the mantle of acquisitive adulthood. She replaced her trust and simple honesty with a grown-up worldliness, and the sophisticated pragmatism that comes with maturity. And she came to view the world with the sad eye of the realist: a bleak and practical world with no magic.

The fairy tales and mystic parables, that had inspired so many of her dreams, were discarded in favour of more realistic and socially orientated writings: the intellectual and literary fashions of her day.

The little girl settled herself - as she had been taught - to the rewards and responsibilities of citizenship. And she grew into a modern young woman, aware of and sensitive to her own important needs and desires; and knowing her rightful niche in the community.

Her life, which had once been so open and inquisitive, shrank into a solid, firmly structured matrix, built entirely around the need for material comfort. In this respect she was a fortunate young woman, for she lived in a time when there was no work for the majority, and consequently generous social benefits to compensate. She had a nice home and car, regular holidays abroad, sufficient money for her comfort and needs, and the time to pursue her own important desires. Any struggle would have to be of her own making.

But she made nothing. In the company of her peers, she sank slowly and steadily, and quite willingly, into the seductive quicksands of mature adulthood. And as those sands dragged her remorselessly ever downward so, beneath the seeming indifferent gaze of the Angel, her spirit gradually died over the years, until finally only her body remained: a firm, lithe, sensual body, moulded to the mood of the time. She was bright, vivacious and socially aware: a most attractive young woman devoid of all childish things, and all childish dreams.

It was a sad story; and there were few that realised. For it was a story of the time, and they were all in that time.

Had they been in another time they might have understood the dangers of this one. She herself might even have understood. For every time has its own individual qualities; its own spiritual tide against which it is folly to fight. Though the rewards can be great.

But the young girl did not fight. Her elders had drawn a veil over her mind and left her only eyes with which to see. So she never saw her adversary.

Before the Story

And she died without ever knowing there was one.

~ ~ ~

All this the Angel knew well

As did the girl
for she had chosen it

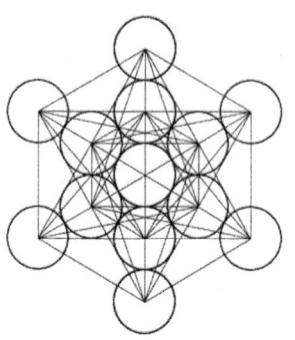

In the Beginning

THE ANGEL finished her story and then walked with the boy in silence, towards a tall, thin building that stood alone at the far end of the sands. Lights twinkled from the high, narrow windows, and they could see tiny dots of people entering and leaving by the small door at its base.

The boy broke the silence. "A pity she had to grow up," he said. "But it was a funny time to choose to live, wasn't it, with all those problems?"

The Angel smiled. "No," she answered. "It was a rather interesting time in fact. It was the beginning of an important change in the lives of all the people on Earth - the time when the seven gifts of its guardian were to be unveiled."

The boy looked at her quizzically.

The Angel explained: "When the Earth was created its guardian endowed it with seven special gifts. But the awareness of these gifts was to remain dormant until the time came when the people of Earth had grown sufficiently to understand them. The little girl's life was the beginning of that time.

"She wanted to experience the early stages of the change - the distant sense of a new age of consciousness gradually, almost imperceptibly spreading its tentacles throughout the dying spasms of the old. In this story, she was freed from the need to work but had lost her child's simple understanding of how to replace it.

"When the gifts are finally revealed, all the people will `become as little children', and regain that understanding.

"The little girl knew nothing of the seven gifts; only that it was a time of important and far-reaching change. You will be living on the Earth shortly after her, but before you go you must learn the secrets of these seven gifts."

The boy was surprised. "But why?" he asked. "I don't think I want to know all that. How can I live a normal life if I learn all that before I go? Nobody else has to. Why do I?"

The Angel turned her face away from his enquiring gaze, towards the darkening sea. A flicker of sadness showed briefly in her eyes. Only when it had gone did she turn back to him.

"We all have things we must do," she explained gently, "and this is something you must do."

"But ..."

"Don't argue!" the Angel interrupted him brusquely. But then her tone softened and she went on: "You will find out why soon enough. Now I am going to show you seven books, each of which contains a story illustrating one of the gifts. You must read these stories carefully, then come to me after each one to show me that you fully comprehend the significance of the gift.

"When you have read all seven, you should understand the purpose of the guardian's seven gifts, and the reason for them being unveiled at this time. Then you will know why you have to do this.

"I cannot tell you what the gifts are. It is important that you find them for yourself."

They entered the building with the high, narrow windows, stood alone at the end of the sands, and began to climb the stairs. The Angel took the boy to a small room right at the top of the building which contained a chair, a table and a single shelf. On the shelf were seven books. She showed him the books and then left.

~ ~ ~

The 1st Gift

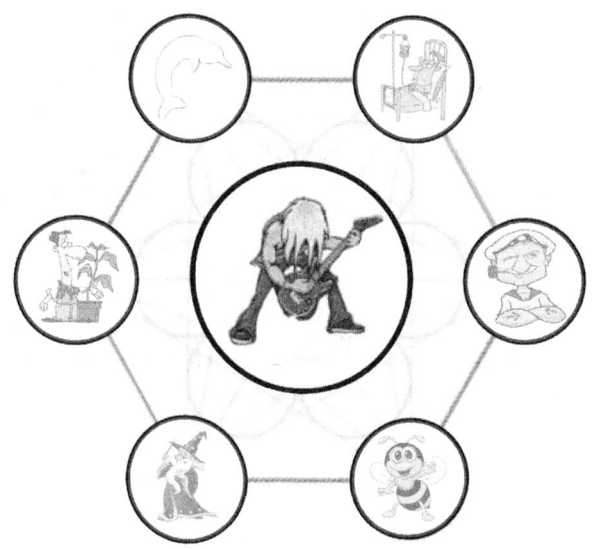

Custer's Last Band

FAR beyond the mountains that encircled the kingdom of the Snow Queen, deep within the swirling high altitude mists forever present in those regions, there lived, in a small cave cleft between two rocks, a retired rock 'n' roll singer called Coalhole Custer. He was a strange man, as befits his calling, with a wild beard and long, flowing yellow hair. His music had been way ahead of its time and so he had retired (not entirely voluntarily), penniless and unappreciated at the age of thirty three, to live alone in the mountains with only the company of a small cat and his thirteen-string guitar.

But Coalhole Custer was content. He had room to

breathe that clean, rarefied air that sparkled forever round the mountaintops, and he had time for his thoughts. The solitude of those mountains freed his mind and let it fly to all manner of strange places, in a way that musicians' drugs had never been able to. He was happy simply to dream his dreams and sing his songs, and allow his restless mind to wander whither it would. And his cat was all the companionship he needed. Those crowds of weirdos that used to surround him at the court of the Snow Queen held no attraction anymore. They had never understood his music and he had never understood them. In truth, he had never even liked them. Trivial was the word that sprang to mind whenever his memories recalled them. He was missing nothing.

On calm summer evenings he would sit quietly outside the cave, puffing on his pipe and gently stroking the cat. He would watch the glowing red ball of the sun slowly sink beyond the twinkling, distant lights of the Snow Queen's city. At times he fancied he could hear music, drifting up on the thermals and attenuating in the thin, clear air far from that city.

Rubbish, he would think to himself; utter rubbish. No idea at all, any of them. Same old emotive diatonic junk: froth for filling meringues – or the minds of citizens. And his cat would purr in agreement, feline disdain twitching its whiskers.

He wrote his music for the mountains now, and for the heavens that seemed so close around him. This was real music, dragged up from the depths of his soul: music that soared above the minds of mortal citizens; that suffused the earth, enveloping it, enjoining it, and drawing it up, rejoicing, to meet the gods that truly made it. For Coalhole Custer knew that he no longer stood alone in the forming of his music.

And in between times he would walk the foothills with his cat, the old thirteen-string guitar slung over his shoulder. In his mouth would be the special thirteen-note Pipes of Pan, built for him by an old radical sculptor who had been banished from the kingdom for carving images of truth. For the Queen's people desired only illusion — shadows behind which they could hide. Even the soil of the Earth was hidden by concrete. The brothels were garnished with fairy lights and the people's faces painted with ochre, their clothes tailored to deceive. Their smiles belied the material machinations constantly occupying their meringue-like minds. Truth was a dream, metamorphosing only in the clean air of the mountains.

Coalhole Custer breathed it in deeply. Down into his lungs and around his heart it flowed, to be formed finally into music and expelled through the pipes, forever in his mouth. And the music of the gods, set free by this man, took wing and ranged all around the mountains, reaching into every crevice and every creeping thing. It filled the plants and diffused into the Earth; it formed into the songs of birds and the whirring of insects, it shaped the clouds. It brought the winds and softened the rain, and reached out for the sun. But it never reached the city.

At that time the city was in something of a turmoil, owing to the impending Coming-of-Age of the Queen's daughter, the beautiful Ice Princess. The trouble was caused by the

Princess's nature, which was as cold as her name. Nothing was good enough in the preparations for the Grand Ball. The decorations — holly plucked from a thousand trees throughout the Queen's domain; castles sculpted from ice; fountains and rare flowers; her name picked out in the lights from ten thousand glow-worms — were tawdry. The specially-made gown — designed by the greatest couturier in the kingdom, assembled by a hundred hand-picked seamstresses from the finest silk of faraway lands — was cheap. The Queen's coach — fashioned from ice of the deepest blue and drawn by twelve golden reindeer, bred for this purpose alone — was uncomfortable. And the band was abysmal.

All the bands were abysmal. The Princess had listened to thirty seven of them, each one worse than the last. "Can no-one write decent music in this God-forsaken land?" she raged. Everyone around her was incompetent. Would anything ever go right in her life? Did she have to do everything herself?

She had the holly burned and a thousand more trees cut down; the castles melted and rebuilt to her own design; the fountains destroyed and the flowers dug into cesspits, along with the glow-worms and the designers. She took a carving knife and hacked the gown to shreds then burnt it, along with the couturier. She drove the coach — with the reindeer — over the highest cliff in the kingdom, to be dashed to pieces on the rocks at the edge of the ocean; then demanded of her mother that a new one be built. And she banished all thirty seven of the bands into the icy wastes of the glacier region, where Snowman fought with polar bear over the flesh of anything that moved.

Finally, on the very eve of the ball, she had the decorations to her taste. The gown at long last fitted properly; and a brand-new coach stood at her door with twelve blue reindeer specially captured by the Queen's Hunters after a fierce and bloody battle with the Warriors of the Tundra.

But still she had not found a band.

The palace was in consternation. The Queen was in floods of tears, and the King had long since gone to visit his brother on the far side of the ocean. The courtiers gathered to hold council.

The Chief Minister presided. "I know of no band left in the kingdom," he said simply. He was ready to resign himself to his fate. He looked around with faint hope at all the courtiers gathered in the Meeting Room but they were all reluctant to catch his eye. For a long while there was uneasy silence; then a young courtier at the back stood up. "I know of one," he said.

The effect was electric.

"Who? Where?" The Minister almost screamed with relief at the prospect of maybe seeing the morrow. "It must be brought here immediately," he demanded. "At once! I will send a battalion of the Queen's Escort to fetch them. Where is that band?" He pointed almost accusingly at the young courtier, as though the whole business were his fault.

"We..el," stammered the young man, now wishing he had kept quiet. It was probably only the Chief Minister who would have had the chop anyway. "Er, it's not quite as simple as that," he said. He explained: "Some years ago I used to play the psychological synthesiser in a band called 'Half a Ton of Nutty Slack', run by Coalhole Custer ...." He paused, brought up by the sudden tension he felt in the room.

The Minister of Technology whistled: "Coalhole Custer! You played with him? That lunatic troublemaker? He's not a musician." The minister felt himself begin to perspire at the very thought of the man. He wiped his brow and calmed himself before continuing: "You must be joking. I can just see the face of the Princess if he appears in the ballroom and strikes up that cacophonous rubbish of his. We'd all be boiled in oil."

There was a strange silence in the room. The young courtier who had confessed to having played with Coalhole Custer quietly sat down, now regretting having opened his mouth. The others stared at him, as though he were a strange being from some foreign land.

"Just a minute," came the testy voice of the Chief Minister. "I don't know much about this Custer fellow, but as far as I'm concerned the Princess wants a band and if he's got one he'll do."

The room erupted in raucous cries of dissent, but the Chief stood his ground. He held his hand up for silence. "If there is no band here tomorrow," he said firmly, "our heads will be impaled on the palace gate. If there is a band, they might not be. So unless any of you know of another band in the country that has not been banished to the Snowmen, we will just have to take our chances with this Coalhole Custer." He looked around for dissent, but the logic of his argument was irrefutable. Only the young fellow who had played with Coalhole Custer spoke.

"Er, he might not come," the young man muttered

diffidently. "He lives alone up in the mountains now, and never has anything to do with the city. He was thrown out if you remember, and I don't think he likes it down here very much."

The Chief Minister smiled unpleasantly. "He will come," he said, in a deceptively quiet voice. There was no mistaking the meaning.

Coalhole Custer sat huddled by his campfire. He poked gently at the embers, stirring up sparks and crackles in the slowly dying fire as he did. His eyes focused quietly on the red flickering in its depths as he hummed a few bars of his new song, as though seeking a reaction in the flames. For a long time he sat there, intermittently humming as he played around with the music, gradually drawing around it some sort of structure. Finally he picked up his guitar and struck a few chords to adjust the tuning; then he began to sing softly to the glow of his camp fire:

> Look into my eyes,
>
> Prince of Darkness,
>
> tell me what it is you see.
>
> Is the Lord of Light in me
>
> or is my soul reserved for thee?
>
> Will you fight the Lord of Light,

Prince of Darkness,
for the soul that lies in me?
Is it worth your while, my Prince,
to save my soul from being free?

My life, O Prince of Darkness,
is it rooted in the Earth?
Will my sanity in whispers
sound around this barren land
in which not even you, my Prince,
have cause for mirth?
Can I walk upon the emptiness
within the nestling void of death
that follows me from birth?
I must delve into your darkness,
look towards the Lord of Light,
and leave the twilight to the Earth.

My life, O Prince of Darkness,

does it lie within the Moon?
Will I bask in silken starlight
as I sway, seduced in sorrow
by the piper's haunting tune?
Can I withstand the sirens
and their symphonies of darkness
that would draw me to the devil spider's loom?
Have I any hope of holding out?
O Lord of Light,
please make the Sun come soon.

My life, O Prince of Darkness,
will it take me to the Sun?
Can I survive the solitude
in all the seas of loneliness
around this race I know that I must run?
Lord of Light, help me survive the race
it seems each time I've won I've just begun.
Hold up for me the hope,

The First Gift

O Lord of Light,
thy will be done.

Look into my eyes, Prince of Darkness,
tell me what it is you see.
Is the Lord of Light in me
or is my soul reserved for thee?
Will you fight the Lord of Light,
Prince of Darkness,
for the soul that lies in me?
Do you think you have the power,
Prince of Darkness,
to prevent me being free?
Lord of Light, I see the night –
please rescue me.
Lord of Light, I see the night ....
Please .... rescue me.

The haunting notes lingered on the still night air, as though addressing themselves to the darkness. The cat lay close to the fire purring quietly, and Coalhole Custer remained quite still, his fingers holding, as though reluctant to leave, the closing chord of his new song.

"I like it," came a familiar voice from close behind his shoulder. The musician whirled round, to face his one-time psychological synthesiser player, now a junior courtier in the Snow Queen's city. They had been close friends in the old playing days, before things had become too hot for the band and Coalhole had been hounded, not altogether unwillingly at the time, to the hills.

"Well, well!" A welcoming grin lit up the guitarist's face. "Psycho! What a surprise. Come and get warm." He grabbed his friend's arm and steered him to the fire, where he rattled up the smouldering ashes and piled on some more logs, along with the kettle.

"Kicked you out as well, have they?" he enquired, when they had settled themselves by the fire.

"No, Coalhole," said the courtier, "but I'm in big trouble, and only you can help. It's the Ice Princess's Twenty-First birthday tomorrow and we haven't got a band. She rejected the lot of them; sent them to the Snowmen. The only band left in the entire kingdom is the old 'Half a Ton of Nutty Slack', and the Chief Minister will personally emasculate me if we don't get it together for the ball tomorrow night. I've found all the others, but we need you. Will you come?" The young man was pleading.

Coalhole Custer grinned. That was original – him being asked to play at an official function. Then he laughed. The

The First Gift

only band left in the land, eh? Whatever his feelings about the Ice Princess and life in the city, he was a musician, and there were interesting possibilities here. He scratched his long yellow beard thoughtfully.

"Does the Princess know that we are supposed to be the band?" he asked.

"No," said his friend nervously. "She might have us all shot when she finds out; but if there is no band, she'll shoot us anyway. So we've nothing to lose." He looked hard at the unkempt figure of the guitarist and crossed his fingers surreptitiously. "I won't blame you if you don't want to do it," he went on. "It's your life and your decision, and anything could happen down there when she finds out, although we've bribed as many of the guards as we can".

"Never you mind about that, Sunshine," said Coalhole briskly, suddenly making up his mind. "Tomorrow night is going to see the first appearance of Coalhole Custer's new band – by appointment to Her Regal Majesty the Ice Princess herself. And it'll be a stormer, believe me – the start of a new musical era." He chuckled and picked up his guitar.

"Rehearsal time, Psycho my old buddy. Let's run through the programme."

The city streets were athrong with people; noblemen and their ladies, Princes and minor Princesses, courtiers, ministers and Royalty from neighbouring lands; all clutching their gold-embossed invitations and wending their way to the ball. The gutters had been whitewashed, and the common people sent out into the fields for the night. The city was clean and tidy, as befitted the Coming-of-Age celebrations of a cold-blooded Ice Princess.

Colourful bunting filled the streets and colourful people the carriages. Trumpeters stood on either side of the Palace steps sounding a fanfare for the arrival of each carriage. The Royal Standard flew from the flagpole. At the top of the steps the Ice Princess stood in her new ball-gown cordially greeting her guests, while backstage of the ballroom Coalhole Custer's new band was tuning up.

Finally, all the guests were received, and the Ice Princess made her regal entry to the ballroom on the arm of a suitably handsome neighbouring Prince. She looked very beautiful; quite splendid in fact, and was rapturously received by all the guests spread around the room sipping champagne. The ranks parted to allow her escort to guide her to a small daïs close by the main stage, which she mounted before turning to the assembled company.

"I thank you all," she said, "for your fine gifts, and I welcome you to this Grand Ball. Let the music begin."

The heavy drape curtains drew back from the main stage and the wild, yellow-haired figure of Coalhole Custer stepped forward. He turned with a smile and bowed low to the Ice Princess. An audible gasp came from her lips and she stared at him, tight-lipped with anger. Belligerent murmurings rumbled from the crowd.

Ignoring their reactions, the guitarist walked slowly into the centre of the stage and surveyed his audience. They glared at him challengingly: the nobility of the kingdom; soon to be sliding slowly beneath a sea of champagne and lust. And why not? the glares implied.

It was their night. A night for pleasure. The night of

the wrong wives. When the guardians of the Nation's morals might forget their own.

The common herd was in the fields; armed guards at the doors. Who need pretend between these walls? The band must conform. Their scowls relaxed into satisfied smiles. The singer dare not censure them.

Coalhole Custer smiled too. Then he turned and addressed the glowering Princess: "Your Highness." He bowed again. "My first song is for you. A celebration of your flowering."

He stepped back, picked up his old thirteen string guitar and slung it round his neck.

"OK!" he shouted. "Let's go. One, two, three, four."

The audience was stunned, as a melody of exquisite gentleness flowed softly from Coalhole Custer's band. It was conventional, beautiful, and totally unexpected. The ballroom was hushed and they all listened, as Coalhole Custer sang:

> You must be sad, my little Princess,
>
> in your boudoir full of incense,
>
> when there's nothing in the world
>
> you haven't tried.
>
> How much d'you have to pay
>
> to get your body through the day?
>
> Have you ever seen your soul, or has it died?
>
> Since this morning's scented bath
>
> not a cloud has crossed your path -

> your life's a crossword
>
> someone slowly fills each day.
>
> Today your hair is fair
>
> and your breasts are almost bare,
>
> for your body is the key that pays the way.

He sang slowly, in a clear, well-modulated voice such that every word was perfectly audible to the Ice Princess and her guests. The Princess stood on the daïs rigid, her face white and set. The guests began to mutter. Coalhole ignored them and continued singing, waving in a little extra bite from the Elephant Tusk Horn Section;

> I grieve for you, my Princess,
>
> safe within your cloud of incense
>
> where you never see the world that's going round.
>
> You'd rather take a bath
>
> than walk the endless winding path
>
> to where the Roller Coaster Road can be found.

The muttering turned into uproar, with guests shouting and brandishing their fists. The guards from the main door advanced on the stage.

Suddenly the singer chopped his hand through the air and the song finished abruptly; on an ill-fitting, expectant note. It caught the attention of the guests and the ballroom went quiet. The guards paused and looked to the Princess for guidance; but she had left.

In the momentary silence, Coalhole Custer's voice carried clearly to all parts of the crowded room:

To you My Friends!

Drunk, drugged, satiated, occult-ridden in the endless hunt for happiness

I give PANDORA'S BOX!

He raised his guitar high in the air and struck a chord that dug deep into the marrow of the watchers' bones, freezing them like a charmer his snake. The sound lingered, as though resonating within the guests. There was something peculiar, almost purposeful, in the manner of its going.

Then the band echoed it, in a wild soaring run of theme and variations that streamed among the spellbound guests like a plague of spiders, spinning webs of music to hold them entranced, and captive before the stage. And on this foundation the musicians layered yet more music until the whole palace trembled in a desperate attempt to contain the ever-rising crescendo of sound. Then they stopped. The sudden silence was almost unbearable.

Somewhere a window shattered, splintering and tinkling to the polished floor of the ballroom. Its faint echoes accentuated the silence. Then Coalhole Custer began to sing, the 'Half Ton of Nutty Slack' filling in behind him to build complex, subtle patterns of strange and oppressive music. It seemed to permeate the very fabric of the palace, reaching out through the walls as though to escape, and Coalhole Custer sang:

> YOU TAKE THE PATH TO WONDERLAND
>
> THROUGH THE DOOR MARKED FORTY NINE
>
> WHERE THE WEREWOLVES LOPE IN MOONLIGHT
>
> THROUGH THE SNOWS WITHIN YOUR MIND
>
> AND THE VAMPIRES RISE TO SWALLOW YOU
>
> IN THE LAND OF UNKNOWN TIME —
>
> YOU'LL NEVER HIDE AWAY FROM WHAT IS TRUE
>
> FOR THE IMAGES REFLECT WHAT LIES IN YOU

Another window broke at the far end of the ballroom and some plaster rattled down off the wall. The music was throbbing heavily now, weird and vaguely out of control. It began to pound at the walls and pierce the windows, trying to break its way out. But Coalhole Custer sang on:

> WHEN SPIDERS CRAWL ACROSS YOUR EYES
>
> AND YOUR LIMBS BEGIN TO SHAKE

WHEN SNAKES SWIM THROUGH YOUR DAYLIGHT

FROM THE DARKNESS OF THEIR LAKE

WHEN REALITY IS DOUBTFUL

WILL YOU KNOW WHICH PATH TO TAKE —

YOU'LL NEVER HIDE AWAY FROM WHAT IS TRUE

FOR THE IMAGES REFLECT WHAT LIES IN YOU

As he sang, oblivious to all around him, his strange music filled the ballroom like an alien entity. It crept into every crack and carving; it ran along the exquisitely moulded lines of plaster that covered the high ceiling; it swirled around the paintings, the icons, the graven images.

Wherever its delicate fingers probed, it drew out resident demons; sucked them from their sanctuaries to be cast helpless and screaming into the spiritual wastes of the ballroom. And as they went they dragged their hiding places with them, pounding the terrified guests with broken images, bricks and dying paintings.

Then it suddenly retreated; permeating the bones of the musicians as though to hide from the horrors it had disturbed. And its alien resonance drove them into a wild frenzy of playing that fed it and strengthened it, charging it with energy from a long and furious run of riffs and discordant key changes that took the musicians to the very brink of their already crumbling sanity.

Then, rejuvenated, like a bolt of lightning it struck

back into the room.

It left Psycho foaming at the mouth, clutching at his psychological synthesiser like a man possessed. The copper triple bass player was kneeling on his instrument in a desperate attempt to stop it levitating, his eyes bulging like balloons. The Elephant Tusk Horn Section was upside down, pumping out a strange, grinding dissonance that seemed to drive the other instruments berserk. The dodo drums appeared to be dancing; pounding away blindly by themselves as the drummer lay flat on the floor in a trance.

Only Coalhole Custer seemed untouched by it all. He stood at the front of the stage dragging indescribable chords out of that old thirteen-string guitar, his long yellow hair flailing in the peculiar breeze that seemed to blow from nowhere.

Then a heavy truss crashed from the ceiling, pinning guests to the floor in a shower of dust and debris. Unable to reach the exit through the jam of bodies, the ones still able to move added their screams to the wild, electrifying music.

And Coalhole Custer sang on:

When the cities fall in ruins

Will you damn the human race

When the sun goes supernova

Will you smile upon its face

And when Armageddon strikes us

WILL YOU CROSS YOURSELF IN CASE —
YOU'LL NEVER HIDE AWAY FROM WHAT IS TRUE
FOR THE IMAGES REFLECT WHAT LIES IN YOU

The music was now clawing at the very structure of the palace, breaking up foundations and vibrating the huge oak roof beams into clouds of feathery dust which filled the air, choking guests and musicians alike. Deprived of support, half the roof collapsed in a roar that almost drowned out the music.

Smoke poured through the gaping hole and Psycho in his frenzy could see Heaven itself, the eyes of God peering through the stars at the carnage caused by Coalhole Custer's music.

And through the smoke and fire, the broken beams and falling bricks, the screams and the running feet, Coalhole Custer's band played on; its manic music whirling around the insane and dying musicians, to pour ever more violently into the shattered ballroom, pounding, hammering, tearing at the nerve-ends; juddering the brain, roaming round the room now way beyond the control of the musicians.

Psycho was lying on his back with one leg in the air, a completely vacant expression on his foam-flecked face. The psychological synthesiser played on by itself, a great steel beam piercing it from above. The copper triple bass player was now airborne, clutching at the curtains as his maddened instrument struggled up through the dust towards the stars.

Small fires had broken out around the stage, licking up

the heavy drapes, but still Coalhole Custer stood firm at the front. His yellow hair was singed and blackened with a smoke that seemed to dance to the unearthly harmonies flowing from his old thirteen-string guitar, which he now held high above his head. And still he sang:

> WITH THE UNIVERSAL LIFE FORCE
>
> OF THE COSMOS AT YOUR FEET
>
> YOU'RE STANDING AT THE CROSSROADS
>
> WHERE THE PLANES OF LIFE ALL MEET
>
> AND WHEN YOU LOOK INSIDE YOURSELF
>
> WHO DO YOU THINK YOU'LL HAVE TO GREET?

Then the demons his music had released turned on Coalhole Custer. As he stood at the front of the stage, his yellow hair plastered with dust and sweat, his chest heaving with exertion as he jerked out the closing chords, he was struck hard in the neck by one of the guards' spears. Travelling with a force that no human could have imparted, it knocked the singer right off his feet, hurling him backwards and nailing him in a cloud of spraying blood to the front of the huge leopardskin bass drum.

The music stopped instantly. Eerie silence fell like a blanket, stifling every tiny sound. Coalhole Custer hung motionless, spreadeagled and dying in the middle of the stage. The tableau was stilled, in a silent snowfall of soot and dust; the only sound the soft crackle of subdued flames. Coalhole Custer's old thirteen string guitar lay on the floor at his feet, where it had fallen.

As the dust slowly settled on its strings it began quietly to play, alone, with no human intervention. The tranquil notes, clear and liquid in their simplicity, curled cleanly upwards through the few remaining rafters, to fall like crystal rain around the dying singer's face.

He turned, slowly and painfully, and peered upwards into the darkness of the night sky, seeking solace. But nothing in all that twinkling darkness, with all its billions of unseeing eyes, could bring succour to the singer. Only the notes from his own guitar, gently weeping down from the broken roof, came close enough to care.

Their lonely tears would frame his last, despairing words:

There - Goes

my

Last - Band

~ ~ ~

The First Gift

Then the singer died,
and a great wrath arose
within the music he had formed.

Around his empty body
discords gathered like storm clouds
sweeping all that was harmonious
before them,

and the stars were darkened
as Coalhole Custer's music
went to war with the very demons
it had itself brought forth.

It was not to bring peace

that

the singer came

The young boy closed the book on the
First Gift

and remained a while with his thoughts

in the lonely tower
at the end of the beach

And the Angel watched over him

Country Garden

THE ANGEL looked up and smiled as the boy approached. She was on her knees raking out a patch of soil near the far end of her cottage garden.

"How do you think the garden is looking?" she called out. The boy sighed ruefully. Nothing in life is ever straightforward, he thought. First the story; now the Angel. Why approach something directly when you can go round the houses; or perhaps the garden in this case. Any faint hopes he had held of the whole business being cancelled when he couldn't find the gift vanished. The Angel would coax it out of him if it took all of Eternity. The gift was in the story somewhere and she would make him find it. The thought was faintly amusing, almost.

"Very nice," he replied noncommittally. He glanced around. It was actually a rather interesting garden: untidy, unstructured, but curiously beautiful; with an air of something slightly mysterious about it; almost magical. He couldn't figure out why.

There seemed to be no order to the garden. Everything was just stuffed into the ground here and there, with no attempt at creating patterns of flowerbeds or complementary sweeps of colour. It was a shambles really, and yet strangely attractive. Some subtle structural notion of the Angel's no doubt lay behind it all. But he couldn't for the life of him see what it was. He walked over to where she was still grubbing around in the soil.

"What are you doing?" he asked. Keep cool, he thought. Let her raise the subject of the gifts.

"Someone gave me a geranium," she said, "and I thought I'd plant it over here where it'll get the sun." She pointed to a little red-petalled flower in a pot by the wall. "Pretty, isn't it?" The boy nodded.

"I think this will be a good place for it," she continued, "don't you?"

It was a casual question, such as anyone might lob into a conversation about plants. But the boy knew the Angel better than that. She was throwing him a line - and he caught it.

"So long as Coalhole Custer doesn't come along and blow it all to bits." He thought he detected the glimmer of a smile on the Angel's face; but she carried on raking the soil and spoke to him over her shoulder.

"Do you think he would?" she asked.

"Well ... I can't think of any reason why he should. But then I couldn't see why he wrecked the Snow Queen's palace either."

"But he didn't," said the Angel. "Why would he go to all that trouble when he could have simply put a bomb in it? And walked away unscathed."

"Well alright," the boy muttered, "he didn't; but his music did. He was responsible."

"Oh yes," agreed the Angel, "he was certainly responsible. But he had no idea of the effect his music was going to have. He had played there before without all that happening - during the time he had lived in the city. And by the time he found out, it was a bit late: his music had grown a life of its own. It responded to the feelings he had put in it.

"But," she finished off, "I think he half expected something to happen."

The boy agreed: "I think he did." Then he took the plunge. "But I don't know what the gift is."

The Angel was unperturbed. "You will," she said. Then she stood up and, taking his hand, walked him off down the garden past the vegetables and fruit trees, the flowers, herbs and shrubs that all mingled in an unexpected harmony.

"Doesn't it look lovely?" she said.

"Why does it look so nice?" he asked her. He sensed a clue here somewhere.

"I don't know," she said. "Look at it. Trees here, bushes there; flowers and vegetables all over the place and in amongst each other. It's a tangle of odds and ends, all mixed up and higgledy-piggledy. There's no order to it at all. I don't know why it looks so nice."

"Mmm," the boy muttered pensively. "There must be some sort of order to it. Order doesn't necessarily mean regimentation though, does it?"

"No," answered the Angel.

"Then presumably you have a good reason for putting everything where you have, even though it all seems haphazard and disorganised." He looked around for an example. "That celandine for instance. Why have you got it growing in amongst that old rubble by the pig sty?"

The First Gift - Angel

"That is the best place for it," said the Angel. "Besides, nothing else would grow so well there. The celandine likes rubbly old ground."

"Well, that's a good enough reason I suppose," said the boy. He looked around for more clues. "How about those herbs in under the wall there? It's a bit stony for plants, isn't it?"

"The thyme and the sage? They like stony ground and must be sheltered from the north winds. They don't like the cold."

"I see," said the boy thoughtfully. And he thought he was beginning to see. "You haven't planted the garden to suit yourself, you've planted it to suit itself." He paused and looked around to confirm that he was on the right track.

"It suits all of us," said the Angel. "It suits the garden for obvious reasons, and it suits me because I like to see it all grow to its fullest potential. Every individual plant in my garden is more important to me than the garden itself; yet if I care properly for each individual plant, they all seem to care for the garden. The result is most effective, as you have observed. You should remember that, because it doesn't work only with gardens."

The boy could see it now: the order in the way that the Angel had put her garden together. Everything was in the place best suited to it, regardless of tidiness. Snowdrops were spread in a white blanket under the trees; a mass of giant burdocks clustered closely around the manure heap and mustard had been planted all about the beehives. Or perhaps the beehives had been set down near the mustard. No matter; the principle was there. Now the new geranium was going in the sunshine.

Everything was in the right place and, because of it, the whole garden prospered. That was what gave the

Angel's garden its strange and indefinable beauty. And a thought occurred to the young boy, which he immediately voiced: "Coalhole Custer's music wasn't in the right place, was it?"

The Angel smiled and said: "Go on."

"Your garden is beautiful," the boy continued, "and lives in harmony with itself, simply because everything is in the right place. The Snow Queen's palace was the wrong place for Coalhole Custer's music, and the imbalance generated some sort of destructive discord between the two. In the end Coalhole Custer's music was presumably the stronger because it grew out of spirit rather than matter."

The Angel nodded her head slowly. "His music was born in the mountains," she explained. "It was created for the mountains out of the spirit of the mountains, and it should have stayed in those mountains where it belonged. In the right place it would have grown strong and beautiful, for it was honest music. It would have inspired and enriched itself and everything and everyone around it, for its honesty gave it great power. In the wrong place its energy was confined and frustrated, and ultimately destructive."

She looked at him, a question in her eyes.

"Space," said the boy confidently. "The right part of it. The guardian put the Earth in exactly the right place; and every thing on it - every rock, plant and animal - was given its own rightful place in the overall scheme of things. That is why and how the Earth works, isn't it?"

"Yes. SPACE was the First Gift to the Earth."

~ ~ ~

The 2nd Gift

7 Days in the Death of Nellie Matilda

IN a small grimy industrial town, far removed from the splendours of the Snow Queen's city, an old woman lay dying in a hospital bed. Further along the corridor, and from which the old woman was equally far removed in a somewhat different sense, a much younger and very pregnant woman was going into labour. Whether there is any connection between these two scenarios I leave you, my long-awaited reader, to decide as the story progresses.

For all that it was a small grimy industrial town its hospital had the very latest equipment and first rate medical staff. The Senior Consultant was greatly respected by his peers throughout the length and breadth of the kingdom and he had brought together into this nondescript little hospital a team of doctors and nurses that was second to no other in the land. Just why this should have happened has no relevance to the story so we shall not pursue it. Suffice it to say that the hospital was the best; and that does have some bearing on the matter in hand.

The old woman's name was Nellie Matilda Johnson, although she had been born an Arkwright. William Johnson, her much beloved husband, had died some two years previously at the very respectable age of ninety-two. Nellie was now eighty-six and very lonely as she had outlived even her children, who had both died sadly young.

But Nellie was not sad as such. She had had a good and happy life with no regrets, and now that the time was at hand for her to depart it she was ready. Not everyone in the Snow Queen's kingdom believed that death was just a doorway to a new world, in fact very few did; but Nellie Matilda Johnson was one of the few. Religion no longer reigned in this kingdom since the onward march of Science had gradually relegated it to the realms of peasant superstition. The development of science under the auspices of the Snow Queen had followed a rather interesting route, having somehow circumvented the discovery of that great watershed in the oh-so-slowly-unfolding synthesis of science and religion that lies buried deep in the destiny of all people. I speak, of course, of Quantum Physics. Without this particular ghost clogging up their materialistic machinery, the Queen's scientists had continued happily along the reductionist road that even dear old Descartes, that doyen of doubt from some other distant Universe, had grown away from since waking from his deathbed to find that he was somewhere else: the blueprint, it seemed, was not in the big toe. One of the results of this scientific sidestep provides us with our story.

We begin on a MONDAY morning, a no more inspiring time for the denizens of this land than for those of any other. Even for Cartesian Reductionists the weekend is the weekend and, weekends being what they usually are, Mondays for them are much as Mondays are for anyone, whichever particular Universe they may inhabit. So Sonia, the nurse who tended Nellie Matilda in the daytime, was not at her best.

"Come on, Nellie!" she grumbled. "You've got to take these pills."

"I don't want any pills," said Nellie wearily. "Just leave me in peace, please."

"But you must take them," said Sonia. "You'll die if you don't."

"I'm quite happy and ready to die," Nellie said calmly. "I've lived my life and it is over. There is nothing left for me here, and it is time now for me to move on."

"Move on?" queried Sonia. "What are you blethering about? I said you'll die if you don't take the pills; I did not say you would move on. What is wrong with this place anyway?

You won't find a better hospital in the land. Now be a good lady and take your pills."

Nellie sighed. "You don't know what I'm talking about, do you?" she said, knowing well what the answer would be.

"No I don't!" snapped Sonia, "and if you don't take your pills I'll call the doctor and he'll make you, like he did last week. You should know better at your age, causing all this trouble to those who are trying to help you." And she scowled, with the smug disapproving look of one who knows best.

Nellie resigned herself to her pills and said no more. The prospect of being force-injected by that arrogant and ignorant old doctor was too much on a Monday morning. But when Sonia had gone she lay back quietly on her bed with her arms down along her sides and closed her eyes. After a moment or two's concentration she climbed thankfully out of her painful old body and set off to find her husband.

"Oh, Nellie," William Johnson groaned, when he saw his wife approaching with that damnable silver cord still attached to her body, "haven't you got away yet?"

"No dear," she replied. "Those maniacs are determined to keep me alive, come what may. You would think they would have something better to do with their time. I can't stop long; it is the middle of the morning back there and the doctor will be doing his rounds shortly. If he turns up and thinks I'm dead, heaven only knows what he will do to me. You know what those types are like if you don't do what they know is good for you. I thought I would just pop over and see how you are; I'm finding it difficult to get out at night now with all these drugs inside me."

"I'm fine," said her husband. "I've got plenty to do, but all the same I am looking forward to you joining me."

"So am I," said Nellie with real feeling, just before the approach of the doctor caused her to disappear, back to whence she came.

Nellie Matilda woke up as the doctor came into her room. She felt that almost irresistible desire to fall back into her dreams that she knew from past experience signified a visit to the new world that she longed so much now to be a part of. Not yet though, it would seem.

"Good Morning, Nellie," the doctor greeted her with a smile. "How are we feeling today?"

"I'm fine thank you Doctor," replied Nellie, "apart from the usual. But there is no point in grumbling to you about that, is there?"

The doctor sighed. He had heard this every morning for the past four months and was beginning to find it rather irritating. Why was it some people could never appreciate what was done for them?

"Nellie," he said in that exasperated tone normally reserved for recalcitrant children, "how can I convince you that we are doing our best for you? Life is precious, Nellie, and we are on oath to preserve it wherever and whenever we possibly can. Besides, I could be sued if I did what you want and the Society for the Rights of the Citizen got to hear of it. Good Heavens woman, you are asking me to kill you. Would you make me a murderer?"

Nellie also sighed, having heard all this before too. She

took a deep breath in an endeavour to calm herself, then tried once more to explain her feelings to the doctor, who was after all not bad, just blinkered: "I am not asking you to kill me, merely to permit me to die with dignity; there is a difference. Because this world rejects religion but fails to replace it with anything else you all think the physical life is the only one. But I know better, Doctor; I have been there, I have spoken with my husband. I know there is a new world waiting for me, and all the beliefs of this life cannot alter the realities of the next. I have finished with secondary school and now wish to go on to the challenges of University; and you would deny me that. How long must I lie here connected to this, being dripped into by that, stuffed to the eyeballs with drugs? I am not a person anymore, Doctor, I am an experiment; no more than a rat in a laboratory. You claim that the preserving of life is sacred. Well, I say this is blasphemy!"

Nellie was now shaking with her suppressed anger, and the dials on the instrument panel above her bed began flickering and gyrating in a most alarming manner. The doctor leaned over and pressed a red button. A few seconds later Sonia rushed into the room clutching a huge hypodermic needle, which she promptly rammed into the wrinkled old flesh of Nellie's upper arm. Nellie quietly passed out.

The doctor wiped his brow. "Phew," he muttered. "That was a near thing; I thought we were going to lose her for a moment there." With a relief that was almost tangible he watched the gauges gradually resume their normal readings. Sonia pouted: "Silly old woman. As if I had nothing better to do than rush in here constantly giving jabs to keep the old bag alive."

This embarrassed the doctor, who in the quiet of his own house could at times be tempted to experience a twinge of sympathy with Nellie's feelings. "That will be all, thank you Nurse," he said in his most formal manner. Sonia sniffed, and flicked her hair back in a minor gesture of defiance before sloping off with the now empty hypodermic clutched in her hand. The daily routine of the hospital reasserted itself; and Nellie's spirit, now trapped in her body by the drugs coursing through her old veins, resigned itself yet again to the daily routine of its seemingly endless prison sentence.

Nellie Matilda finally awoke from her drug-induced haze just in time to say her prayers before going to sleep again for the night. She closed her eyes and placed her hands together, just as she had every previous night for some eighty-odd years, except that now she could not get out of bed and kneel as she felt she ought. Although it was not her fault, it still grieved her.

'Dear Father, I'm weary; I've lived out my life. Please take me at the end of this day; I so long to come home. Dear Father, please take me home.' Then Nellie, worn out from her day, fell asleep; releasing her spirit for a few short hours to the love and tenderness of her husband.

On TUESDAY morning Nellie Matilda did not wake up. The nurse in panic called the doctor, who was mystified to discover that all the instruments at the old woman's bedhead were reading correctly. She was not dead, yet no amount of shaking and shouting would wake her. In the end they resorted to electric shock treatment, which did jerk her convulsively into wakefulness; although it was fully half an hour before her eyes focused properly and she was able to speak.

"It was just as if she wasn't there, even though her body was in the bed and seemed perfectly normal," Sonia said to her friends during the morning tea break. "It was real spooky, especially after the way she is always rambling on about going to a new world." And the nurse shuddered at the recollection of the old woman's vacant face.

"And d'you know what she said when we told her we'd had to electrotherapise her to get her back alive again?" Sonia added. The other nurses looked suitably blank so she furnished the answer: "'Oh dear God, why cannot these people let me go in peace?' Weird I call it". And she stirred an extra sugar into her tea to calm herself. Really, this old woman was getting too much, she thought. I shall have to ask for a transfer.

The doctor was feeling equally frustrated over the behaviour of Nellie Matilda Johnson, although he expressed his frustrations rather more eloquently than did his nurse, as he discussed the case over coffee with the senior professor.

"I do not understand it, Charles," he said. "I have investigated every organ and every system in that woman's body and can find not a thing wrong with her. Yet she slides away steadily day after day, despite all the drugs we pump into her. She will not eat, and we have to force feed her with a number of drips. What with that and the electronic hookups required to monitor her condition, due to her frequent and irregular relapses for no apparent reason, she looks more like a terminal cancer case than a perfectly fit and healthy woman. She may be fairly old but there is plenty of life left in her yet. The whole business is a complete mystery to me. If I was not a rational, scientifically trained doctor, I could almost believe that she is deliberately and consciously willing herself to die."

The old professor smiled enigmatically. "Perhaps she is," he said. "I do believe there is a possibility that such things can happen. There are a number of surprisingly well-documented cases amongst primitive peoples with strong religious beliefs, you know." He got up and went over to the urn to refill his coffee cup. "Is she religious?" he asked the doctor over his shoulder, as he carefully stirred in one level teaspoon of brown sugar.

"Yes," the doctor replied. "She is forever going on about being ready to move onto the next world. But surely Charles it is not our business to get involved in that sort of mystical claptrap? We're doctors, and our job is saving lives: keeping people alive. Whatever the ins and outs of religion it is not for us to just let people die. Besides, we would get sued if anyone found out. And, anyway, how can a person possibly will themselves to die? I cannot believe that."

The professor reflected for a while. "I fear, David," he said finally, "that our material world and the spiritual world, if one accepts that such a thing exists, do not make comfortable bedfellows. There was a time, a long while ago, when science and religion co-existed fairly happily as most scientists then had some form of religious belief. The development of science has disproved so much of what the old religions believed in that no self-respecting scientist of today would entertain the merest whiff of religious ideas.

Speaking personally, and off the record, I am an old man and I have travelled a lot and read a lot, and I must admit – between these four walls, mind – that I am not wholly convinced of the current scientific viewpoint. I suspect that there is more to this life of ours than we think."

The professor paused and took a mouthful of coffee, then continued: "As for the particular case of Mrs Johnson, however, the only professional advice I can give you is: keep giving her the tablets. Then you have at least protected yourself from the risk of litigation."

Mrs Johnson went to sleep early that night. But before she did, she put her hands together and prayed: 'Dear Father, I'm weary; I've lived out my life. Please take me at the end of this day; I so long to come home. Dear Father, please take me home.'

WEDNESDAY was bath-night; or to be precise, bath-very-early-in-the-morning. Poor Nellie was woken just before six, given her breakfast, then treated to the dubious pleasure of a blanket bath. This was hard work for the nurses as Nellie was paralysed below the waist so could not move at all. Why she was paralysed, no-one knew, as the doctors could find nothing physically wrong with her. Anyway, the old lady bore it all with her usual stoicism and was shining clean for when the ward sister did her rounds.

Sister Newman was a plump, kindly, middle-aged lady, brimming over with common-sense. Although she was not what one would call religious, she had been in nursing since her teens and had seen a great many people die. She had also known a few who had died briefly then come alive again, and every one of them had recounted more or less the same tale – of walking towards a bright light and being filled with an overwhelming sense of joy, only to hear a deep voice saying: 'It is not time for you yet, you must go back', whereupon they woke up to discover that technically they had died for a few minutes.

Sister Newman was not especially imaginative, and certainly not prone to an uncritical belief in everything she heard or even experienced, but there was something about these tales, something about the simplicity of them and the similarity between them, that had bequeathed to her a more open mind on the matter than most of her colleagues possessed. So she had more than a little sympathy for Nellie Matilda's feelings.

"How are you my dear?" she said warmly, as she bustled up to Nellie's bedside. Nellie smiled. She sensed the concern in the Ward Sister's voice, and could also see it in her eyes. "I'm fine thank you Sister," she replied, in a voice that was undeniably sad and yet just a little chirpier than when she spoke to the other members of the nursing staff.

The sister felt her pulse and looked her over carefully, but took no notice of the blinking lights and dials above the bed. Deep in her heart she knew what ailed Nellie, although her professionalism prevented her from admitting it to anyone; even Nellie, although they both knew that she knew.

She turned and looked out of the window. "It is a nice day, Nellie," she said. "Would you like me to organise someone to wheel you out into the garden for a while?" She expected a negative reply. They had all resigned themselves to the fact that Nellie showed no interest in anything, other than the hope of dying as soon as possible. But this morning she was surprised.

"Yes," Nellie replied unexpectedly, "I think I would like that."

There was no reason for anyone to know, of course, but it happened that it was Nellie's wedding anniversary that day. One of the pleasures she and her husband had shared was taking a simple walk in the country on a nice day, and she had a sudden urge to draw that memory back to her.

"I'll send a porter shortly, Nellie," Sister Newman said, "and we'll organise you some warm clothes as there is still a little nip in the air."

So later that morning Nellie was wheeled out into the hospital garden, where she was left to sit in the sun for an hour or two before lunch. It was a spring morning, slightly chilly as yet but bursting with new life and vibrating with that particular freshness that occurs at no other time. Nellie breathed deeply of the sparkling air and closed her eyes to listen to the bird-song and bring back memories from her life. And suddenly she found herself walking along a road that she could not see, towards a bright distant light that seemed to fill the whole world with joy. The bird-song changed to angel-song and Nellie's heart leapt as she realised that at long last she had shed her mortal strife and was walking, fit and young again, into her long-awaited new world.

She was dimly aware of voices rising above the angel-song. William? she wondered, and called out his name, over and over and over as the light seemed to fade ahead of her and she began to feel a fuzziness in her head and the new world began to disintegrate all around her .....

She was still calling for her husband when her eyes opened back in the hospital bed and she realised where the voices had been coming from. "We've saved her!" she heard the doctor cry out.

And when the end of that long long day finally came and the evening drew on to her time to sleep, Nellie Matilda placed her hands together and with tears streaking her tired old cheeks she prayed: 'Dear Father, I'm weary; I've lived out my life. Please take me at the end of this day; I so long to come home. Dear Father, please take me home.'

THURSDAY was visiting day, although no-one ever came to see Nellie. And at the end of the empty day she would place her hands together and pray: 'Dear Father, I'm weary; I've lived out my life. Please take me at the end of this day; I so long to come home. Dear Father, please take me home.'

On FRIDAY the doctor examined her again, and left as bemused as ever. Her paralysis had spread upwards to her neck and the only thing she could do now for herself was pray: 'Dear Father, I'm weary; I've lived out my life. Please take me at the end of this day; I so long to come home. Dear Father, please take me home.'

SATURDAY was a strange day, full of memories for Nellie. Suddenly, after being alone in the house through all the days of the week, the rooms seemed full of people. One husband and three children may not constitute a crowd but somehow they filled that house with warmth and laughter and fun. The atmosphere was quite different to that of a Sunday which was a quiet and peaceful, reflective, contemplative sort of day. Nellie enjoyed them both equally, although in different ways. Saturday, she felt, belonged to the world she lived in; but Sunday swirled with hints of a wider world: a world that only as she grew older did she gradually come to recognise as being just as real as the one in which she currently lived.

Saturday in the hospital was a sad day for Nellie, when the loss of her family weighed most heavily upon her, when she felt most lonely. She always tried to get away and visit William but it was not easy with all the bustle in the hospital. Often she would close her eyes and lie for hours trying to get away from her body, with no success. At such times she would pray through all the day: 'Dear Father, I'm weary; I've lived out my life. Please take me at the end of this day; I so long to come home. Dear Father, please take me home.'

SUNDAY was perhaps the saddest day of the whole week; the day in which thoughts of the wider world that Nellie Matilda longed so much for welled up into her heart with greatest force. There was a time when the Parson would visit all the patients on a Sunday, but in those secular days of the Snow Queen's reign it was not deemed right that religion should be foist upon the people, so the Parson never came. There was a time when hymns were broadcast on a Sunday morning, but that had been stopped too. There was little for Nellie to do on a Sunday but pray: 'Dear Father, I'm weary; I've lived out my life. Please take me at the end of this day; I so long to come home. Dear Father, please take me home.'

On MONDAY Sonia, the nurse who tended Nellie Matilda in the daytime, was not at her best.

"Come on, Nellie!" she grumbled. "You've got to take these pills."

"I don't want any pills," said Nellie wearily. "Just leave me in peace, please."

"But you must take them," said Sonia. "You'll die if you don't."

"I'm quite happy and ready to die," Nellie said calmly. "I've lived my life and it is over. There is nothing left for me here, and it is time now for me to move on."

"Move on?" queried Sonia. "What are you blethering about? I said you'll die if you don't take the pills; I did not say you would move on. What is wrong with this place anyway? You won't find a better hospital in the land. Now be a good lady and take your pills."

Nellie sighed. "You don't know what I'm talking about, do you?" she said, knowing well what the answer would be.

"No I don't!" snapped Sonia, "and if you don't take your pills I'll call the doctor and he'll make you, like he did last week. You should know better at your age, causing all this trouble to those who are trying to help you." And she scowled, with the smug disapproving look of one who knows best.

Nellie resigned herself to her pills and said no more. The prospect of being force-injected by that arrogant and ignorant old doctor was too much on a Monday morning. But when Sonia had gone she lay back quietly on her bed with her arms down along her sides and closed her eyes. After a moment or two's concentration she climbed thankfully out of her painful old body and .....

The boy stopped reading, confused suddenly. He was sure he had already read that bit. He riffled back through the pages, and discovered that he had been reading a verbatim repetition of Nellie Matilda's first Monday in hospital. There must be a printing fault he decided, so he flicked on a few pages, looking for something new. But Nellie's second week seemed to be a word-for-word clone of her first.

He sat back and thought about this for a little while, then gradually the significance of it dawned on him. He smiled warily, uncertain whether to be amused by the writer's ploy or saddened by the old lady's plight. Then, curious, he turned to the last page to see how it finished.

But he could not find the last page. Every time he turned over, expecting to find it, he found the story continuing as ever. Even when he flipped backwards from the end cover he still ended up in the middle of the story, which went on just as before when he attempted to read on again to the end.

Baffled, the young boy put the book down on the table and stared at it for a while. It must have an end, he thought; it is of finite size, therefore presumably of finite length. It was not as though the last page simply petered out, there just was not a last page. However often he turned what seemed to be the last page he found another, and the story went on and on; every week identical to the previous one.

    Then suddenly he grinned. It must be a subtle joke of the Angel's, a dig at the Queen's scientists' inability to discover Quantum Physics. She had constructed the book in such a way that he could not observe the end, and thus collapse it into reality.

    But what if Nellie was real? What if he was seeing in print something that was actually happening on the Earth? And his failure to observe the end to Nellie's misery was preventing that end from coming about.

    No, he decided. The Angel did not play silly games like that with people's lives. If the story was happening, then he was viewing a version of it in which something was very wrong; in which something essential was missing from the very fabric of Nellie's existence. And that something must be the clue to the gift.

~ ~ ~

The young boy closed the book on the
Second Gift

and remained a while with his thoughts

in the lonely tower
at the end of the beach

And the Angel watched over him

The Journey

THE BOY finally closed the second book having given up all hope of finding the last page. What could be missing from this version of the old lady's life, that could in any way be related to a gift? He felt little wiser than when he had opened the book. He had hoped to find this second gift in time to spend the day fishing as the weather was so lovely, but the chances now seemed very slim. Feeling rather fed up with it all he went in search of his tormentor.

The Angel smiled as he approached looking thoroughly glum. "Come on," she called out encouragingly, "let's go for a walk. It's a lovely day and I've got something to show you."

The boy sighed, but he tagged along dutifully. What could this gift be? he wondered. Ordinary life? No, he didn't think so. Death perhaps? But how could death be a gift? Maybe it was. He shrugged. Doubtless the Angel would winkle it out of him eventually.

She took his arm companionably and steered him along the lane out towards the open countryside. After about ten minutes' brisk walking they emerged onto the bank of a river.

A fishing river, the boy observed ruefully. Its clear, fast-running water tumbled and glittered over a gravelly, rock-strewn bottom that he could see quite plainly. Tall willow trees drooped their shadows over the rippling surface, their leaves almost kissing the swirls of deeper pools by the bank. The water wound around the trees, rushing headlong for the open sea. But despite the hurrying noise of the river it was a peaceful place - there was a special sort of quiet under those stately trees.

They turned upriver and sauntered slowly along the grassy bank, taking in the sights and sounds and smells of the riverside. There was life here. The boy could feel its vibrant energy surging beneath the blanket of peacefulness surrounding them. But beneath the Weeping Willows it was quiet by the river. A background tinkling of water falling over rocks was studded with the occasional sound of a distant bird, the irregular plop of fish jumping.

The water was so clear the boy could see the fish, swimming along close to the bottom. There were quite a number of them, all making their way upstream, tails swishing lazily against the current.

"Salmon and Sea Trout," said the Angel, following the boy's gaze. "They are coming home to spawn."

The boy looked up sharply. Did he detect a clue? Was this what the Angel wanted to show him? But she said no more until they rounded the next bend in the river and came to a weir, where the water tumbled and fell three or four feet down a craggy face of splintered rocks. In the foam and spume that filled the air, the boy could see more fish, flying in desperate leaps as they tried to scale the obstacle and reach the calmer water beyond.

They stopped by the weir and watched for a while the trout and salmon struggling to fling themselves over the cascade of water, clear of the rocks and into the next stretch of river. Some reached it and some failed.

"Every year," said the Angel, "without fail they battle their way up this river, past nets and fishermen, over weirs and waterfalls, just so they can spawn in the same place they came from. Many of them don't make it; but still, each year, they come in their thousands to find a mate, and lay their eggs in the shallow upper reaches where they themselves were born. Then they die; leaving their eggs to hatch alone.

"When the eggs hatch, the fry head back to the sea, facing even more dangers than their parents had. The few that survive to maturity then make the long journey all over again, back to the very same river in order to lay their eggs. And with that done, they die. Every year is the same."

The Angel turned away from the quiet struggle going on in the river and continued her stroll along the bank. Her companion remained watching the fish for a little while, thinking about all this, before finally running to catch her up.

"A bit like the old lady," he said, a shade breathless. "Dying when her time on Earth was up."

"Yes," agreed the Angel, "much like that."

"Only they wouldn't let her die," added the boy, "even though she had lived her life and was ready to move on."

"They wouldn't." The Angel gave away nothing and they walked on in silence, the sound of the river now muted by the rustling of a light breeze creeping around the branches of the trees.

The boy was still thinking about all this when they

reached the final stretch of the river - the shallow gravel beds where the salmon spawned. Here was a frenzy of activity - a boiling melee of fish churning almost to a froth the water that was barely deep enough to contain them.

The females were busy scooping out shallow redds in the gravel - nests in which to lay their eggs. Around them male fish fought and jostled to get in position above a female so they could mate. As each female dropped her eggs into the redd, the male covering her sprayed them with his milt. The fish then washed a protective covering of gravel over the fertilised eggs with their tails, before swimming away to die.

In the midst of this frantic, all-consuming activity smaller fish were darting about, snatching up and eating eggs before even they reached the gravel; while younger salmon hid beneath their big sisters, adding their sperm to that of the rightful mates above. Practising, perhaps.

As he watched spent, emaciated fish drifting away downstream, uncaring, their thin bodies tearing on rocks and stones, the boy thought again of the old lady in the story. No doctors to stop this lot, he thought.

The Angel broke into his reverie. "Look at them," she was saying. "Torn, diseased, starved and exhausted from the journey; they've had enough. But they've done what they came to do. Now it's all over; and they can die in peace.

"Can you imagine," she went on, "battling all this far; struggling over weirs, evading fishermen and poachers, fighting otters and the like, your quest so urgent you even fail to eat, then finding that the river is endless? That you must follow it forever, fighting and starving all the way, yet never reach the spawning grounds? Never reach the end of the struggle?

The Journey

"Can you imagine a life with no attainable goal? No end? No death to bring peace when the time comes?"

"That," said the boy, visibly shaken, "sounds like a vision of Hell."

"Exactly," said the Angel. "And what is it that saves the salmon from such a fate? What is it that would bring peace to the old lady in the story if the doctors didn't meddle? What is it that enables cycles to begin and end? And begin again? What is it that prevents us from being imprisoned in crude, material bodies for all of Eternity? What brings all things on Earth to a close?"

"Time," said the boy quietly.

"Time," echoed the Angel. "TIME was the guardian's Second Gift to the Earth. Time to live; and when living's done, to die. Time to learn; and when learning's done, to die. Time for toil and strife; and when that is done, to die. Time for dying; and when that is done, to live anew.

"Time brings change. It begins and ends all things. With the gift of Time, we can now safely live on Earth, knowing that all things must end. Knowing always that one day we will return home.

That is the secret of the Gift of Time."

~ ~ ~

The
3rd Gift

Charlie's Angel

FAR away at sea, many miles from the land of the Snow Queen, a small sailing ship was battling for survival in a fierce winter storm. Deeply laden with pearls and spices, silks, precious metals, artefacts and all manner of aphrodisiacs for the nobles of the Snow Queen's court, the little vessel was struggling to round the notorious Cape of Storms. It was the dead of winter and she was beating hard against a full gale to try and squeeze through the narrow gap left between land and ice-cap.

And the wind had shifted as she stood close inshore for

a favourable eddy in the current. A scant five miles off the coast she had found herself suddenly on a dangerous lee shore. Instead of battling to round the Cape, she was now battling to avoid being blown onto it; onto the jagged rocks that fringed that inhospitable coastline, far too close, yet invisible in the wild blackness of that howling wintry night.

High up on the swaying yardarms snow and sleet whistled out of the darkness to clutch at the seamen's frozen fingers, as they fought to subdue flogging, ice-laden canvas. The ship was overwhelmed. Sail had to be furled and lashed to the yards before the screaming wind ripped the masts out of her. If it did, that would be the end. To stay off the shore, she had to keep sailing, somehow.

Great creaming waves hissed and tumbled out of the night, roaring like thunder, to curl and break in torrents on the heaving decks. The little ship staggered and struggled to pull herself free of the tons of foam and spuming water which roared the length of her decks, ripping away stanchions and lockers as it went. The men working in the waist leapt for the lifelines, hanging on grimly as each wave washed over the ship. As it poured away, spent, through the open scuppers, the men would drop back to the deck and heave away again on the braces, trying desperately to trim the few remaining sails to the wind.

All through that long nightmare the seamen worked without pause — trimming braces and sheets, heaving on buntlines and securing frozen gaskets round sails that were as stiff as wood. And all the while the wind screamed incessantly and plucked at their hands and oilskins like a living creature. And the sea plucked at the ship, flinging her here and there like a cork.

Throughout it all the Captain stood alone on the windswept poop, numb with tiredness. One arm was deep in the pocket of his oilskin, the other hooked firmly round the weather mizzen rigging. It was the second night of the storm and he had not moved since it began, save to gesture orders to the Mate. It was impossible to shout against the screaming wind. Impossible almost to move. Impossible almost to breathe at times.

In twenty four hours, he estimated, they had struggled perhaps half a mile from the coast, most of that at the beginning of the first night, before the storm had reached its full ferocity. Now, he thought they were losing ground. It was hopeless to try and navigate in those conditions. Only his years of experience enabled him to sense the ship's progress. And it was that experience which had kept his ship and his men safe for the last twenty four hours.

No-one could calculate which sails to set, which course to steer; which waves to drive into, which to ease her over gently. No formula could tell him when to push and when to give a little. He had to feel, sense the delicate balance which would keep the ship off the shore without smashing her up against the inhuman forces of wind and sea.

He stood alone, apparently oblivious to the wind that screamed and dragged the very breath from a man's mouth; oblivious to the waves that reared out of the blackness and fell in great swirling, foaming torrents onto the deck of his tiny ship; seemed barely to notice the faint, drifting cry of a man dragged bodily from his grip on the yardarm, blown away like a feather into the inky nightmare around them.

While the Mate and his men fought in that hellish wind to control flailing, murderous canvas high up the masts, the Bosun's party struggled grimly on deck, up to their armpits in swirling water, to handle braces and sheets and keep the few remaining sails trimmed so that the little ship would sail. The Captain stood apparently unaware; thinking, feeling and hoping.

Four men fought with the huge wheel, trying to steer and trim the ship to just the right angle with the wind and sea; tried to feel out that delicate, indefinable course that just might take their ship and her crew to safety.

The Bosun remembered it all vividly, right up to that big wave. There had seemed a strange lull in the wind and he had looked up from the deck, into the blackness to windward. But it was no longer black. Reaching almost to the truck of the mainmast, barely a ship's length away, breaking, foaming, cascading like a torrential waterfall, gleaming white with hundreds of tons of boiling spray and spume and water, was a wave. The eternal nightmare of every mariner, it was the chance meeting of perhaps a dozen wave-trains, each crest piling atop the others till the weight of water could no longer be sustained.

Momentum brought the top of it curling over to fall on the game little ship. Masts, yards and sails splintered and crashed to the deck. The pilothouse ripped from its coamings and was smashed out through the bulwarks. Hatches and deckbeams caved in under the sheer weight of water, and broken men floated like dolls in the swirling foam. The Bosun was washed clear through a gaping hole in the bulwark and never saw his ship again. His last sight was the Captain still standing, unmoved, on the poop.

All this was still sharply etched in the mind of the old Bosun as he lay in the darkness on what felt like a sandy beach. Waves washed over him, but they were small ones — expended remains of ocean growlers that had broken themselves against the land elsewhere. Miraculously, he was somewhere sheltered, somewhere hidden from the rocks that he knew fringed the shore that had been to leeward when the ship went down. He lay there in the darkness for a long time, spluttering occasionally as a wave passed over his head, but unable to move. He gave thanks to God for his deliverance then passed out.

When he awoke it was daylight. The clouds still tore across the sky, but they were breaking up into patches of blue. The wind was easing, and gradually shifting to blow off the land. It was turning into a nice day.

The Bosun felt carefully all over his body and was relieved to find that, apart from a few cuts and bruises, he had escaped the wreck unharmed. He sat up gingerly and looked around him. He was lying on a small stony beach between two headlands, beyond which he could see just the wild sea, tumbling away into the distance. He appeared to be in the lee of something. An island perhaps?

Inshore of the beach was a scraggy cliff tufted with sparse grass. That was all he could see. There was no sign of any life, not even seabirds. All inland away from the storm, he decided. Perhaps there were houses and people. With this hope he pulled himself wearily to his feet and headed slowly towards the cliff, looking for a pathway that would take him to the top. He was too exhausted for rock-climbing.

The Bosun was no longer a young man, but neither was this his first shipwreck. What he lacked in strength he made up for in experience and resilience. In his own gentle way he was a tough man; as so many gentle people are. He had learnt that himself, over the many years he had spent in fo'c'sles of ships trading far and wide for the merchants of the Snow Queen. The Captain he had just watched go down, standing calmly on his poopdeck, had been such a man — a type found so often at sea. A gentle, unassuming man, with a backbone of steel; firm when he had to be, and scrupulously fair. His first concern had always been his ship; his second his men. For himself, he took nothing.

And now the Captain was dead, along with most of his men. Drowned while carrying silks and satins home for preening princes and courtiers. But these thoughts no longer angered the Bosun. The contempt he had felt for such men in his youth had turned, over the years, to pity. He and the Captain were the lucky ones, he reflected, to have such clarity of thought as only the sea could give. To see life in its simple forms, uncluttered by all the confusion of riches and social graces; and the obligations and blindness they create. The Captain had found peace, and so, one day, would he.

The Bosun found himself on an island — a few windswept acres of scrubby moorland, surrounded by the white-flecked seas. Way in the distance he could just see the high peaks of the mainland, as unattainable as Heaven itself. But he was too old a hand to let the disappointment hurt. Shelter and food were the immediate essentials, and he set out to explore his new home: a home, possibly, for the rest of his life. To think of this island as a home was a natural reaction to the old sailor. All his life home had been the particular ship he had been on. In the absence of his ship, this desolate little island would do. It wouldn't occur to him to see it as a prison – that was the city.

Dusk found the old Bosun comfortably ensconced in a brushwood shelter, a rabbit roasting over the fire. He leaned contentedly against the pile of firewood, whittling himself a simple spear with the seaman's knife that had survived with him. Beyond the crackling of the fire he could just hear the muted roar of the surf. The sound of the sea made him feel more at home. He was lucky. It seemed highly unlikely that anyone else had survived. Why he should have done he didn't know. He simply accepted it.

Later, with the rabbit reduced to bones that he carefully preserved for making into fish-hooks, the Bosun drank his fill at the nearby stream, then stretched out peacefully on a bed of old leaves. To a shipwrecked mariner it was sheer luxury. He closed his eyes and fell into the deep, untroubled sleep of a child.

The next morning was clear and windless. As he wandered the island searching for firewood, the Bosun could see that they were no more than about three miles from the mainland. This was a busy trade route and he might well see a passing ship working its way through the straits on a quiet day. Hopeful of possible rescue, he spent the day building a huge bonfire with which he could signal a distant ship.

So the days passed for the Bosun; hunting and fishing, making clothes from the skins of animals he caught, and adding bit by bit to his bonfire. But he saw no ships.

He had been on the island about three weeks by his reckoning when he first saw the skua. It was a Great Skua – a big brown bird like an overgrown seagull, but with the cruel hooked bill of an eagle. Whether it was looking for a place to nest, or just over from the mainland hunting, he didn't know. He saw it circling the small colony of seagulls that lived in a stubbly patch of ground at the far end of the island. He often visited the colony to collect a few eggs as a change from his usual diet of fish and rabbits.

He stood and watched the skua for a while, circling low down over the squabbling gulls. Then it dived, disappearing behind the steep grassy bank separating him from the gull colony. There was an almighty rumpus as gulls flew off in all directions, squawking and screaming. The Bosun knew that skuas were predatory birds, not above snatching the odd baby seagull, so he dashed across to see what was happening.

As he topped the rise he could see the bulky brown shape of the skua with its huge wings open, leaping up and down stabbing and pummelling a small seagull. The gull lay on the ground flapping its wings feebly, mewing like a cat. The Bosun ran down the hill shouting and waving his arms. As he got nearer, he stooped to pick up a stone and hurled it in the direction of the marauder. It missed, but the bird was alerted. When it saw the irate Bosun approaching at the run, arms flailing, it backed away hissing, head low down like an angry goose. Then it opted for discretion and took off, winging away in the direction of the distant mainland.

When the Bosun reached the gull he saw that it was badly injured and bleeding, so he picked it up and quickly wrung its neck. Then he saw the egg nearby. The gull must have been trying to protect it from the skua. He reached down and picked it up to take home for his tea. But as he turned away, the sight of the dead mother made him pause. She had given her life to save that egg; it didn't seem right that he should simply take it home and eat it, as the skua would have done. That made him little better than the seagull's killer.

He felt the egg in his pocket; it was very warm. The mother had obviously been sitting when the skua arrived. It was right, he felt, that the baby should live, after its mother's sacrifice. He wondered how near it was to hatching. He thought for a moment, then came to a decision. Picking up the body of the dead mother, he turned and walked rapidly back towards his camp.

It would be something to do, he thought; something more interesting than simply sitting around waiting to be rescued. He had never heard of a seagull being reared from the egg, but there was always a first time. All he had to do, he reasoned, was keep it warm.

He soon reached his camp and entered the lean-to hut he had built out of branches and driftwood. Dropping the dead gull on the floor, he went straight to the smouldering fire and stoked it up. He placed the still warm egg in a deep nest of dry leaves close to the fire and covered it with more leaves and earth. Then he sat back, wondering how long it took a seagull's egg to hatch. Not that he knew when it had been laid, or the incubation period for that matter. But at least it gave him something hopeful to look forward to.

The egg stayed warm, and three days later it started cracking. By the evening a baby seagull had hatched out, and the Bosun was fussing around like an old grandmother. The fluffy little chick crouched in its nest and yowled for food. But the Bosun was ready.

On the offchance of the hatching being successful, he had kept the head of the mother seagull, and he now used it to feed the baby. The red spot on the beak, he knew from past study, was a trigger that made the baby open its mouth for food. The mother would then regurgitate half-digested fish into the baby's open mouth. The Bosun did the same; chewing fish until it was like paste, then poking it through the beak into the chick's mouth with a little stick. And it worked.

The baby thrived; and it grew. The old Bosun seemed to spend the better part of every day stuffing food down that gaping, clamouring mouth. But he was happy; glad to have saved the baby whose mother had died for it, and glad to have something to do other than morosely watch for ships that never came. And Charlie, as he had named it, was good company. He grew very fond of him.

When Charlie was a little bigger the Bosun began taking him round the island on his foraging expeditions. The young gull would perch on his shoulder, peering avidly about it, yelling at the other passing gulls, and occasionally falling off. But he made no attempt to join the others. The Bosun was his mum; and he showed his devotion by pecking constantly at the old man's ears.

But the affection was mutual. What was a sore ear, thought the Bosun, compared to friendship?

In the evenings they would sit round the fire together eating their supper. The Bosun had carved some wooden bowls now that Charlie was old enough to feed himself, and they each had their own. Charlie's was filled with chopped up fish, while the Bosun's would vary. Sometimes he had rabbit, sometimes fish; occasionally just seaweed and fruit. But he never had seagulls' eggs again. And he didn't bother any more to look for ships; his life on the island now seemed quite sufficiently meaningful. With Charlie's company the Bosun was content.

Even when Charlie began to fly and went off fishing by himself, he would still return to the old Bosun's hut of an evening to share a little of his supper, and perhaps his company. But they spent less and less time together now that Charlie was independent of his mum. And before long, the Bosun knew, Charlie would be away to a new life as an adult seagull. He was already spending most of his days flying with the other mottled young gulls; swooping along the wind currents that were drawn up over the cliffs, and scouring the beaches for food.

The Bosun began to think again of rescue. He spent more and more days wandering the cliffs and, where at one time he would just have watched Charlie, he now scanned the distant horizon for ships. And he rebuilt his old signal fire, long since pillaged to feed the fire in his hut.

At night he would dream of the sea and ships, even of land and the civilisation of the Snow Queen's kingdom. He dreamed of the family and friends who now presumably thought him dead. And one night he dreamt of his old Captain: the man he had last seen standing calmly on the poop watching his ship break up and sink beneath him.

Only it wasn't the Captain he saw in his dream, it was

Charlie – Charlie speaking with the Captain's voice. It was Charlie stood on the poopdeck in the screaming wind and spray, as the Bosun and his men fought with the frozen halyards, each crashing sea filling the deck and rising to their necks. And Charlie spoke to the Bosun, the voice of the Captain rising clearly above the howling gale.

"Do not worry, my old friend. You will be saved; from this storm, and again from the island you will be swept to. You have more years yet in which to suffer this world.

"Tomorrow at noon you must light your signal fire, for a ship, homeward bound to the kingdom, will pass just below the horizon at that time. The crew will see your smoke and come for you.

"And do not fear for me."

The Bosun awoke with a start, the dream still fresh in his mind. He looked towards the spot by the fire where Charlie normally slept, but the seagull was gone.

He shook his head and thought about the strange dream. He had never believed the superstition that the souls of drowned sailors lived in seagulls. Could they? No, it was wishful nonsense.

But as the sun neared its zenith he had almost finished preparing the bonfire. Damp leaves and twigs were piled high on top of it to make smoke, so that it would be visible further in daylight. He felt a little foolish, but then there was no-one around to see. Why not have a bonfire? It was something to do. And he couldn't know that there wasn't a ship passing below the horizon that day.

All through that long afternoon he stood on the edge of the cliff, peering out to sea. Behind him the bonfire gradually died to a flicker. By nightfall there was just a pile of smouldering embers, and he had seen no ship. When it became too dark to see, he turned and trudged wearily back home to his little hut.

Charlie, who was normally ensconced by the fire long before dark, was nowhere to be seen. And by the time the Bosun was preparing for bed, he had still not appeared. He worried about Charlie, sufficiently to be able to forget the failure of the signal fire. That night he slept fitfully, dozing, then springing awake at the slightest sound, hoping it might be his little seagull. But when he finally dragged himself out of bed with the dawn, there had been no sign of Charlie.

It was a tired and saddened old man who half-heartedly ate a small breakfast of fish. After he had eaten he savagely kicked soil over the fire, ground it out with his heels and stamped out of the hut to begin a thorough search of the island. He hoped he might find his little friend with perhaps just minor damage to a leg; something he could fix. It seemed odd, he pondered as he walked, how Charlie had disappeared immediately after his strange dream. A dream that obviously had been just wishful thinking on his part. But something seemed to have happened, to break the harmony of his simple life with Charlie and the island. He felt depressed, and that was unlike the Bosun.

He rounded a small clump of wizened trees and stood looking down on to the bay where he had first washed ashore. In the middle of the bay, at anchor, was a sailing ship. A small gig was being rowed towards the beach and the Bosun could see an officer, quite clearly, standing in the sternsheets.

He fell to his knees on the wet grass, put his hands together and cried out thanks to God for his salvation. Then, with tears streaming from his eyes, he ran — all thoughts of Charlie gone — down the steep path towards the beach.

The Bosun leaned on the rail of the little ship, clad in fresh clothes and puffing contentedly on a pipe. The Mate was alongside him, recounting all the latest news of the kingdom. Above the ship, unnoticed by either of them, a seagull soared on long white wings, round and round, ignoring all the others that squabbled in the scraps thrown over by the cook.

"...... palace was razed to the ground," the Mate was saying. But the Bosun didn't hear him. Now that he was safe on the ship he was thinking of Charlie again and wondering what had happened to him. He had asked the Captain to scour the island for his friend, but it seemed the time could not be spared. They had already lost a day and a night coming for him, having seen the smoke the previous afternoon. And that had set him wondering about his dream.

But dream or no dream, he was desperately sad at leaving without saying goodbye to Charlie. The little seagull had been a good companion during all those months on the island — months that would have been intensely lonely without Charlie.

The Mate was still talking.

"No-one knows what happened," he was saying, "but the Ice Princess has been in the foulest of moods ever since. Something to do with the band, I believe. I tell you, the kingdom is no place to be these days; you'd be better off staying ......"

He was cut short by a scream from somewhere above their heads. Then a seagull smashed into the deck at their feet in a flurry of blood and feathers. Its neck was pierced with the bolt of a crossbow, and blood poured from the wound, swirling around the seamen's boots like a red tide. The Mate stared horrified.

But the Bosun turned cold. Ice ran down his spine and into his heart as he knelt and cradled the dying Charlie in his arms. Charlie looked at him with surprisingly calm eyes for a long time, then suddenly fell lifeless in the Bosun's shaking hands.

Tears streaked the old man's rugged, lined face as he slowly rose to his feet, gently holding the dead body of his friend in strong seaman's arms.

"Good shot eh?" came a cheery cry from behind him. The Bosun turned unseeing, his eyes blurred with tears. But the Mate saw.

At the break of the poop stood a grinning merchant, on board to keep an eye on his wares. His ermine-trimmed robe ruffled in the breeze and a crossbow swung negligently from his right hand. His round, puffy face looked pleased.

"Scum!" spat the Mate, who knew full well where the souls of drowned sailors went. The Bosun turned to him – a kindred spirit.

"Take me back to the island please," he said.

~ ~ ~

The young boy closed the book on the
Third Gift

and remained a while with his thoughts

in the lonely tower
at the end of the beach

And the Angel watched over him

Gone Fishing

IT WAS soon after midday when the Angel entered the room. The young boy was sat at the desk staring rather glassy-eyed at the third story, which still lay open in front of him. He felt tired and fed up. There seemed to be all sorts of possibilities in this one. The gift could be almost anything - love, eternity, hope, life; anything. He could not sort out which one.

He did not seem to be doing very well so far. He felt sure the Angel would soon despair of him. Whatever it was he had to do on Earth, he was beginning to think he was just not capable of it.

He swivelled in his chair at the sound of the door opening, and was surprised to see the Angel standing there. He shrugged his shoulders apologetically.

"I can't seem to figure out this one at all," he said, with a sigh. "There are so many alternatives. What is it?"

The Angel shook her head slowly. Yes, I know, he

thought, I must work it out for myself. "I'm tired," he said with some feeling.

The Angel smiled. "Never mind," she said. "Forget about that for today, I think you have had enough. Let's go fishing." And with that she turned and left the room.

The boy could hardly believe his ears. Fishing! His tiredness vanished and he flew out of the door.

The Angel's boat bobbed alongside the wall of the tiny harbour, varnish and yellow paint glinting in the afternoon sun. She was a sturdy little open boat some eighteen feet long, fitted with a small two cylinder diesel engine, and a stumpy little mast and derrick just abaft the foredeck. Under the derrick was a capstan, driven by rods and gearing from the engine, for hauling the little wing trawl that lay neatly flaked in the stern of the boat. A small wooden trawl door hung from each quarter.

The two of them climbed aboard the boat, started the engine, and motored slowly out of the harbour. The Angel stood at the tiller and, once clear of the entrance, she set course for a patch of clean trawling ground where she knew they would find some big plaice.

The boy sat perched on the gunwhale, his face wreathed in smiles as the little boat rose and fell to the waves. It was a beautiful day: clear and warm with just a light breeze to ruffle the water. A day to be at sea.

He breathed in the clean, salty air and listened to the gentle chuckle of the bow rippling through the small waves. The diesel engine thumped away steadily and the Angel leaned back in the sternsheets, steering with one arm draped over the tiller. The boy was happy and the Angel content. But then she always was.

They soon reached the grounds and shot the gear away downtide in about four fathoms of water. The Angel set the boat on course and throttled the engine so that they were making a steady two and a quarter knots over the ground. Then she handed the tiller to her young crew and went to check that the warps were vibrating evenly, showing that the doors were properly on the bottom and dragging the sweeps through the muddy sand, rooting out all those dozing plaice.

"Digging well is it?" enquired the boy. The Angel nodded.

"It always intrigues me," the boy continued, "how you can sense, just by feeling the vibrations in those warps, exactly what is going on down there."

"Well," said the Angel, "when the doors and the net are set properly, you get steady, even vibrations from both warps. That tells you the doors are churning nicely through the sand, keeping the sweeps on the bottom; and the angle between the warps shows how far out the doors are flying.

"I know from experience what the warps feel like when we are catching well, so if there is any difference then something is wrong. The door might have toppled, or a sweep caught up round its G-link, or maybe even the net has rolled over - which can happen if you shoot away across a strong tide. If there is hardly any vibration at all, the door is not on the bottom - not enough warp out usually.

"It's all part of the general awareness a fisherman needs when he is at sea. You should know about that - all the things you need to be constantly judging and sensing: the state of the sea; strength and direction of wind and tide; any looming change in the weather; your position and course; how the engine is behaving; how the gear is working. That's why fishing is so interesting. To me anyway."

She glanced casually at the boy, then added: "But you find real contentment at sea, don't you? Why?"

That stumped him for a moment. Why did he? Was it peaceful? Not usually. Restful? Only occasionally, and certainly not when fishing. Just pleasant perhaps? Sometimes, he decided; but all too often it wasn't. When the wind howled and waves rolled aboard high enough to slop down your neck; with the gear hitched up round a rock on a black night in a rising gale, fish boxes crashing around in the water that swirled over the bottom boards; and you couldn't see where you were and home seemed a long way away; when you were scared and wondered whether you would ever see that home again, then it was not pleasant.

No, there were complex reasons, he decided, for the contentment he felt at sea. And he remembered a night, running home before a gathering storm, with broken black clouds racing across a starry sky. His little boat was under sail - a tiny storm jib for'ard - and she felt like a living thing, roaring and surfing down the faces of the cresting waves, the spume blown off by the wind and glinting silver in the starlight. Then she would sink into the following trough, hidden from the wind by the next wave he could see climbing against the sky, and everything would go quiet until that next wave picked them up and bore them skywards, back into the ceaseless blast of the wind.

He had clung on to the tiller, wet and miserable, desperately trying to steer a safe course down through those waves. And he had looked at the blackness around him - squinting his eyes against the driving spray - and there was no living thing anywhere. In all of existence there had seemed only him and the wind and the waves, and the stars.

Up above him, dodging around the fleeing, fractured clouds, were countless billions of stars; some near and some far. Some, he knew, no longer existed; yet he could still see them. Some were about to die, yet he would see them for many years to come. And he wondered how many were there, whose light had yet to reach him.

That was not a sky above him, it was a lamination of time. Layer upon layer of different slices of time, reaching out beyond his vision, beyond his comprehension.

He had felt very small, and singularly aware of the sheer enormity of existence and his own tiny part in it. Beneath that indescribable, endless vista of time and space - and who knew what else - there was a young boy and his boat, battling for their lives in a storm; unbeknown to anyone.

But perhaps not? Perhaps someone was up there, watching over him. It was a comforting prospect; and of no less value for that.

That experience, he remembered, had made the nightmare of the storm worthwhile. That vision - of the timeless immensity of life; the billions of other worlds, on which perhaps other young boys in small boats battled for their lives in unimaginable alien storms - had remained with him long after he had reached the safety of harbour.

And now it had come back to him. Awareness, the Angel had spoken of - essential to a fisherman; to any seaman for that matter. That was why he liked being at sea. He had a sense of awareness out there - of his own being and its relationship with others. He was conscious of life and death; of feelings and senses; conscious of values. And that, he suddenly knew, was why the Angel had brought him fishing - to remind him of that consciousness. For Consciousness, he realised, was the third gift.

He turned to the Angel, who was leaning over the transom checking the tension of the warps.

"The third story is about awareness, isn't it?

Awareness of one's own life and the lives of others. Awareness of relationships; needs and fears, love and sorrow. Awareness of space and time; events; death, and what lies beyond it. Awareness . . . consciousness.

"I think the third gift was Consciousness."

"Yes," the Angel confirmed, straightening up from the transom. "CONSCIOUSNESS was the guardian's Third Gift to the Earth.

"The first was SPACE - in which it could exist; the second was TIME - through which it could change; and the third was CONSCIOUSNESS - by which it could know.

"These first three gifts give the Earth form and structure, enabling it to create a suitable environment in which people can evolve and then grow. The remaining four define its future, and give the people their purpose." Then the boat stopped dead, the trawl warps twanging in the water astern of them. The boy grinned.

"I think you've just found us a rock."

"Oh well," the Angel sighed. "I should have been aware of that, I suppose." She laughed. "Let's haul the gear then and see if we've caught anything for our tea."

~ ~ ~

The
4th Gift

Flight of a Honey Bee

Henry was a small, anthropomorphic honey bee. He had a startling black and yellow body, covered with hairs for trapping pollen, and four hard-working, whirring wings. He also had five eyes, two feelers, six legs, three skins, four lips, four Malphigian tubes, two mandibular glands, two salivary glands, eight wax glands, three body segments, a very large multiple brain, and a sting – among other things. He was, for all his apparent insignificance, a complex little creature. He was also – being a worker bee – technically a 'she', although sexually undeveloped. However, Henry was an aggressive little honey bee, always buzzing around, shouting and telling the other bees what to do; which masculine trait explains both name and pronoun.

Whenever a worker bee returned to the hive after a hard day searching for nectar, she would perform a ritual dance to show the others where the best nectar was. Henry was always around at this time, and the moment he deduced from the dance where the nectar was he would zoom off at great speed, cussing and buzzing, little wings whirring madly as he strove to get ahead of all the others. If another bee tried to overtake him, Henry would peel off like a fighter-bomber and attack from above, buzzing with fury. Henry always got to the nectar first.

The other bees grew fed up with Henry, and one day they sent a deputation to the Queen Bee, asking her to get rid of him. If she could trap him inside one of the empty cells in the hive, they said, they could all gang up and cement him in with propolis. He would die slowly and painfully from suffocation.

But the Queen Bee was a good and just Queen. She knew that two wrongs did not make a right. However unpleasant Henry might be, it would not do the other bees any good to behave in the same way. It was better that they should attempt to pull Henry's behaviour up to the level of theirs rather than allow him to drag theirs down to the level of his. This advice, however, worthy though it was, turned out to be rather theoretical; which is to say that all efforts to achieve it failed miserably.

Something clearly had to be done about Henry, before the other bees took the law into their own hands. The Queen Bee had tried speaking to him personally about his behaviour, but he just did not seem to realise (or want to realise) what he was doing. He wanted to be first into everything, and that was that. The Queen did not know what to do about him.

Finally she decided to go to the Snow Queen for advice. The Snow Queen was very fond of her bees, and even fonder of their honey. She did not want anything upsetting them and reducing her harvest. And she had little patience with anything, or anyone, that prevented her from getting what she wanted.

"That darned Henry," she scowled, for she knew him well. He was a menace whenever she went out into the garden, always buzzing about and getting in her way. If he had not been such a good worker she would have sprayed him with pesticide long ago. She could well understand him upsetting the other bees. Worker or no worker, she could happily dispense with his services, for a little while at least. Mind you, her dislike of Henry was reciprocated – he would get in an absolute frenzy when she chased him with the fly-swatter. "And all I'm doing is going about my business," he would grumble. There was no love lost between the Snow Queen and Henry the honey bee.

But the Queen had an idea for removing him for a while, something that would utilise his energies and at the same time give them all a little peace in the garden.

She decided to make him the pilot of a space probe that the kingdom was launching the following week. Its mission was to explore a strange planet far away on the other side of the galaxy, and return with as much information as it could. They had failed to learn anything about it from their telescopes, as all the signals they had directed towards it had returned exactly as they had left. It was as though the planet were a huge reflector.

The mission would take a very, very long time. Henry would be the ideal pilot. And it would settle the discontent among the other bees.

And so it was.

With Henry blasted off into space, life in the beehive became peaceful once more. The Queen laid her eggs, and the workers scurried about collecting nectar and pollinating the flowers. They soon forgot about Henry.

Henry sat in the control room of the tiny spaceship and twiddled his wings. He was bored. There was nothing for him to do all day but check the instruments and rework the occasional calculation. And he was lonely, with no-one to shout at or bully. He wished he was back in the hive. That abominable Snow Queen had a lot to answer for. He would get his own back on her one day.

And so the days passed, so many of them, and Henry sat in his control room twiddling his wings and staring at the passing stars. They all looked the same. Everything looked the same. Henry was fed up.

Then finally one day the little space-craft began slowing down. Henry leapt to his feet and stared out of the porthole. Right ahead of him was a planet, that grew larger even as he watched. This must be it, he thought. His little hairy black and yellow body quivered with excitement. Something to do at last. Someone to talk to?

It was an odd-looking planet. He couldn't make out any discernible features at all. It was almost like a sketch – a rough outline. But it was there. He would soon find out all about it, then he could get off back home where he belonged. He would buzz that Snow Queen till she went mad. It was a pleasant thought.

Very shortly the spaceship landed, and Henry climbed out to have a look round.

Strange, he thought. He couldn't actually see anything. It was not that he was blind; he could see all right. He could see his spaceship, and he could see his boots. But he could not see anything on the planet. No hills or streams, no flowers or birds, no grass, not even any ground. He couldn't actually see any planet, and yet he knew he was on it because there he was, standing right next to his spaceship. It was very odd.

Any other honey bee would probably have gone back to the spaceship and sat down with a cup of tea to think about it. Not Henry.

He looked around him, then bellowed at the top of his voice: "What the hell's going on here, then?"

The reaction was both unexpected and violent. Henry found himself lying flat on his back with a deep, booming voice reverberating in his ears:

"What the hell do you think is going on here?"

Henry came up buzzing angrily, fists waving in the air; shadow-boxing, for there was no-one there. He stood still for a moment, mystified, and glared around him. But there was no-one to be seen, not even a planet. There was just Henry and his spaceship, perched on a planet that he could not see. And somewhere a voice, that must have come from something he also could not see. He felt a tiny shiver of, not quite fear, but something close to it.

But Henry was no coward. He squared his shoulders defiantly and called again:

"Who the hell are you, anyway?"

He was back on the ground, ears ringing with pain.

"Who the damned hell do you suppose you might be?" the voice was saying slowly, in harsh, biting tones.

Henry was frightened now. This was quite beyond his ken. But he was also angry. And he could see a large stone lying by his hand.

He leapt to his feet and grabbed the stone, then hurled it mightily in the direction he thought the voice had come from.

"Cop hold of that then," he yelled, and braced himself for a reply.

For a very long moment nothing happened. Then he heard the voice, low and menacing:

"I did, and you can have it back."

Henry felt a crash on the back of his head; stars flew round in his eyes, then he fell to the ground unconscious. The spaceship watched him, but said nothing. As did the little man.

Henry came to lying on the ground where he had fallen. His head felt as though he had run into a brick wall, and his temper was not one bit improved. He sat up and looked around him. Nothing; not even the planet that his feet told him he was standing on. Just the spaceship standing there, silent and impassive.

He looked at the spaceship, then stared hard at it for some minutes.

That's it, he thought. That's it! His eyes gleamed with sudden recognition. Then he jumped to his feet, pointing at the spaceship.

"You!" he yelled, his voice quivering with anger. "You're the culprit. Those blasted bees rigged all this, set me up for you. Just 'cos they don't like me." He cast around wildly for another rock to hurl at the spaceship. The little bee was shaking with rage. The spaceship sat on its legs, unmoving and unmoved.

Then the voice returned.

"Here's a rock, you stupid little cretin." The voice was laughing at Henry, who stood rigid, rock forgotten, staring at the spaceship. But the voice did not come from the spaceship. Its next utterance made that chillingly obvious.

"Here's a nice big rock," the voice chortled maliciously. "Throw it at your spaceship. Wreck it. Then you'll be stuck here forever."

Henry could feel a large boulder pushing its way into his hand. He stood stock still, petrified, willing the thing to go away.

The voice cackled.

"Lost your bottle, Henry? D'you want me to throw it for you? I'll smash that spaceship into a thousand pieces, then there'll be just you and me, for all eternity. What d'you say, Henry?"

Henry found his voice.

"Please," he pleaded. "Please don't. I want my spaceship. I want to go home. I'm sorry if I've upset you. I promise I won't do it again." He collapsed into a flood of tears.

"Don't cry," said the voice gently. "No-one will hurt your spaceship, or you. I'm sorry I spoke so harshly to you.

You are welcome on this planet."

It was a few moments before Henry registered what the voice had said. And the way it had said it.

But he missed its sincerity. Which was a pity.

Damn thing's taking the mickey, he thought. Nobody takes the mickey out of me.

Henry slowly turned round and stood, hands on hips, staring into the empty nothingness from which the voice had seemed to come.

"Are you taking the mick?" he growled, truculent as ever.

The voice laughed: a cold, cynical laugh with no humour whatever. It was no longer gentle.

"Taking the mick?" it snorted. "Out of you? A big tough honey bee like you? Just because you were on your belly, grovelling and snivelling like a baby? Why should I bother taking the mickey out of a cowardly little squirt like you?" The laugh was chopped abruptly.

Henry's anger now was cold and malignant.

"I'll throttle you," he snarled, his voice rising with his fury. "Show yourself you little rat, and I'll ki ....." His words ended in a strangled gasp. He could see nothing, but strong hands were round his throat, squeezing the life out of him.

Henry struggled, desperately trying to free the invisible grip from his throat. He buzzed his wings and hit out with his arms and legs. But the grip just tightened. He felt himself go dizzy. Henry knew he was going to die, and with that last thought in his head, he blacked out.

"You don't learn, do you?" the little old man said, not unkindly, when Henry woke up. Henry shook his head and looked around him.

"Am I dead?" he quavered.

"No, you're not dead," said the little old man. "Just a bit hard to teach, that's all."

Henry looked at him, then at his spaceship, then back to the little old man. He started. The old man looked real. It was the first thing the worn-out little honey bee had seen since arriving on that dreadful planet.

"Are you real?" he asked, in bewilderment.

"Yes, I'm real," the old man replied. "I live here. I'm the only living thing, nay the only any thing on this planet. In fact," he went on, "even the planet isn't really here. There's only me. And those, like you, who visit."

Henry was taken aback. He must be the voice then, he thought. But that didn't make sense. How could that weedy little old man be The Voice? Someone was playing tricks on him. He began to feel annoyed, and was about to shout at the old man, when something seemed to click in his little brain. He fought down his temper, glancing anxiously around him. It had suddenly dawned on him that it was his anger that seemed to rile The Voice. He didn't want any more of that.

He looked at the old man. He was a very ordinary, featureless sort of little old man; there was nothing about him you could actually describe as such. He was just a little old man, and he was there. That was all Henry could say. He couldn't think of anything at all to say to the little old man. In fact, he was decidedly wary of opening his mouth at all. It seemed to have brought him nothing but trouble every time he had done. So he just stood and looked at the little old man, and waited for something to happen.

For a long time a rather worried little honey bee and a featureless little old man stood on a planet that wasn't really there, and gazed at each other. Which was fine for the little old man as time had no meaning for him. It was also fine by Henry, who was determined not to initiate anything ever again while he was stuck on this weird planet. In fact, he would think twice about initiating anything ever again wherever he was. Who knew where that voice could reach? Way across the Universe to his beehive, perhaps? The possibility worried him. He tried to be casual. Why should he care who got the first lot of nectar anyway? It didn't really matter very much, did it? And he decided that it was really rather boring buzzing the Snow Queen. In fact, there seemed a lot to be said for simply being pleasant.

The little old man spoke.

"Are you learning, Henry?"

Dumbfounded, Henry nodded. What was this little old man? What was this planet, anyway?"

"I am the only person unaffected by the qualities of this planet," the old man went on, as if half in answer to Henry's unspoken question. "The planet as such does not exist. Neither does anything on it. Nevertheless, it can be felt. You can land your spaceship on it, and walk on it, as you have done. And yet it does nothing. It neither grows nor moves, nor lives nor dies. It circles nothing and nothing circles it. And yet it has purpose. You have seen that purpose."

Henry nodded. "I think I have," he said. "It seems to, sort of, shout back at me every time I shout. And when I was sorry, it was kind, and I thought it was taking the mickey, so it did. It seems to sort of reflect what I do. Is that right?"

There was no brashness in his voice, no trace of annoyance.

"This is the Land of Mirrors," the old man said. "It reflects the qualities of everything that happens to it. It has no identity of its own. If you are angry with it, it will be angry with you. If you are kind to it, it will be kind in return. All those who come to the Land of Mirrors see only themselves. Did you like what you saw, Henry?"

"No," said Henry humbly.

"Then neither will others," said the old man.

"Yes," said Henry. "I see what you mean."

"You must learn to behave to others," said the old man, "as you would have them behave to you. That way you can all live peaceably."

Henry nodded. "There's logic in that," he said.

"Well, if you've learnt your lesson," said the old man, "then it's time for you to go home."

"Good idea," said Henry. "There's someone I want to see back there. On second thoughts, perhaps you should see her." And off he went.

Two weeks later Henry arrived home. He had quite enjoyed the return journey, watching the stars buzzing past his porthole. And he had pottered about happily doing his checks and calculations. He felt distinctly at peace with the world as he stepped out of the spaceship to a tumultuous welcome from the citizens of the Snow Queen's kingdom. And then the Queen arrived.

She did not bother saying 'Hello' or 'How are you?', and Henry could see greed written all over her face before she even opened her mouth. She did not disappoint him.

"Well?" It was more a demand than a question. "What's it got? Minerals? Diamonds? Gold? Furs? Skins?" The Queen's eyes glinted as she reeled off the list.

I should have expected all this, thought Henry. It must have been his new-found good nature that made him surprised. It was certainly his new-found good nature that stopped him being rude.

"Does anyone live there?" the Queen went on. "What have they got? Spices? Silks? Weapons? How many battlecruisers would we need to conquer them?"

Henry did not quite know how to handle this, so he said nothing. Which, of course, absolutely infuriated the Snow Queen. She turned puce.

"Come on, bee, out with it!" she yelled. "What did you find out about the place? Do I have to drag it out of you? Can't anyone do a decent job of anything round here except me?" That gave Henry an idea.

"I didn't find anything," he said simply. There was a horrible silence. He thought the Snow Queen was going to literally explode. But finally she managed to snarl out some words.

"What do you mean 'Didn't find anything'? What's the matter with you? You're an imbecile, a cretin. I send you all that way at vast expense and you come back here and tell me you found nothing." The Queen was beginning to get a grip on herself. "Why," she finished, dangerously, "did you find nothing?"

"Well," said Henry calmly, "as you say, I'm a cretin and an imbecile; just a simple bee whose job is gathering nectar. That is a very complex planet with a difficult approach. It needs someone with far more intelligence than I have to explore it."

"Damn you," said the Queen, "do I have to do everything round here myself?" Henry barely suppressed a little smirk. "You're fired, bee. Get back to your hive and be thankful I don't spray you on the spot." She turned on her heel and stalked off.

The next day a very angry Snow Queen blasted off for the strange planet accompanied by her friend the Queen Bee and a heavily armed squadron of battlecruisers. Two weeks later astronomers in the kingdom observed what seemed to be a massive stellar explosion in the vicinity of the strange planet. They noted it to tell the Snow Queen on her return.

But the Snow Queen and her squadron of battle-cruisers never returned. Which, although not surprising, was a pity, as they may have been intrigued to discover that that complex and aggressive little character, Henry, had been renamed Henrietta. And the Queen's Beemaster was plagued with an outbreak of laying workers: somewhere in the now queenless hive was a worker bee that had developed sufficiently strong feminine tendencies to begin laying eggs. This was a nuisance to the Beemaster as the colony would not now accept a proper new Queen; but it was food for the thoughts of others.

~ ~ ~

The young boy closed the book on the
Fourth Gift

and remained a while with his thoughts

in the lonely tower
at the end of the beach

And the Angel watched over him

Leaning on a Gate

THE BOY leaned quietly on the little white-painted wicket gate leading into the Angel's garden. He watched her carefully hoeing around the bean plants in her vegetable patch, which was kept as beautifully as the rest of the garden.

It was a magical garden this, tended so affectionately by the Angel. A hotch-potch of flowers, fruit trees, shrubs and vegetables, with old roses and clematis roaming willy-nilly around them all. Honeysuckle and ivy almost covered the far wall, hanging in beautifully untidy loops around the front door of her cottage, and the air was filled with a fascinating mixture of scents - lavender and rosemary mingling with the clambering honeysuckle, the stocks and the jasmine. And lying behind these, the fainter aromas of apple blossom and a variety of roses.

In and around the wafting, drifting scent of the flowers was the gentle hum of bees going about their tasks in the garden - flitting, buzzing methodically from flower to flower, gathering nectar and spreading the essential pollen. The air seemed filled with a wild array of colours, given movement by the light swaying breeze and the constant flickering of black and yellow as the bees meandered across the boy's vision.

In the background, and far above the garden, he could hear the undulating trill of a skylark, singing its private counter-melody across and through the soft cooing of doves roosting in the nearby trees.

The varying sounds and smells, the contrasting colours, the shapes and patterns in the garden, even the Angel herself, all seemed to harmonise into one great swirling sensual array that, far from battering the boy's senses, seemed to flood through them like a tide, building to a crescendo then ebbing away quietly to leave him refreshed and at peace. He felt a part of it all himself, drawn by the primroses and sweet peas, the bright brave daffodils, the sombre, elegant columbine; entwined and bound by the ramblers and creepers, drugged by the bewitching scent of the honeysuckle, snared by the siren-sound of the bees.

No sign of Henry here, he thought with a smile. Or perhaps he had already returned from the Land of Mirrors. Certainly there was nothing to disturb the harmony of this garden. Even the surrounding trees and the compost heap were constructive in shaping its balanced form. A myriad different shapes and smells, colours, sounds and purposes mingled and blended to form one magical whole. Would that the Earth were like that.

But he knew that very soon it would be. For the fourth gift of its guardian was surely Harmony: a gift whose seeds, even now, were beginning to sprout in the fertile soil of that world, a living matrix potentially infinitely more splendid and exciting than a thousand Angel's gardens. He looked up and caught her smiling at him, and he knew at once that he was right. The guardian's Fourth Gift to the Earth, and the first stage of that world's unfolding purpose, was HARMONY.

~ ~ ~

The 5th Gift

The Philosopher's Stone

One lovely spring day a philosopher was strolling through the woods, pondering on the questions of the time. And they were confusing times in the land of the Snow Queen, especially for an old, traditional philosopher like him.

For seventy years now he had lived in that kingdom, most of his time spent on the only quest that need ever concern a true philosopher — the interminable struggle to understand the purpose of his own existence. Why he should live. Why he should live here. Where this curious thing called human life came from; and where it was going to.

He certainly didn't like the direction it seemed to be

The Fifth Gift

going in now. His years of quiet contemplation had been thrown into turmoil by the rolling waves of technology now sweeping across the kingdom. Questions that had once occupied him for months of deep solitary thought followed by weeks of complex discussion with colleagues, now seemed to be answered at the press of a button. His world was full of winking lights and buzzers, spewing forth rationalised explanations that the half-baked intellectuals confused with truth.

Yet even he, with no technological or much scientific background, knew that these computers were only very fast adding machines. How could they have intelligence, as their acolytes claimed? How could bits of copper and mica understand things unfathomable to the finest human minds? He didn't like it; not least because it undermined him.

Life was not easy for a philosopher at the best of times, but at least when he had first taken up the game it had had a certain kudos. A philosopher had been respected in those days. Now, people's minds were filled with computer logic and their bodies covered with digital gadgetry. They rushed from one astounding technological breakthrough to another, inventing machines to do everything they needed and much that they did not. No-one had time to sit and discuss things with the philosopher any more.

Besides, they all thought the Universe was a vast cosmic computer, and men mini ones, so what was there to discuss anyway? He couldn't even get his books published any more. Who was going to read 'Significant Aspects of Astrological Synchronism in Relation to a Nine-Dimensional Universe' when it was next on the bookstall to 'Sizzling

Nights of Computerised Lust in a Dinosaur's Den'? Not many. He could understand his publisher's reluctance.

So he had taken to strolling through the woods and communing with the trees. At least it was quiet and peaceful out there. And he felt at times that the trees knew more than the computers. He was particularly fond of the big old oak trees, their simple permanence representing a stability for which he constantly yearned. He sometimes wondered whether perhaps they knew it all; that all knowledge, in some strange way that men could never understand, was encapsulated in those strong flowing branches, the odd, crenellated leaves; drawn up in the sap from the Earth herself. For surely the Earth must possess knowledge to make the greatest of all thinkers seem mere schoolboys; and perhaps the way to it was through her soil.

There was one particular tree he had always felt close to, and he would often sit at its base in the warm sunshine, lean against its trunk and soak up the tremendous energy that he sensed flowing incessantly upward, into those twisting, growing branches. He always felt rejuvenated after this.

This particular day, however, he stopped in a small clearing and lay down with his back resting comfortably against a large rock. The rock was rounded and smooth, seeming to grow from the very ground as it nestled snugly in a bed of mossy grass and fallen oak leaves. The sun shone down through the overhead branches, warming the old philosopher's face as he gently closed his eyes and tried to dispel all thoughts from his weary mind.

"I wish I had a brain like yours", said the stone, quite

The Fifth Gift

clearly and distinctly, the moment the philosopher's mind was empty. The old man sat up with a jerk, and looked to see where the sound had come from. He felt niggled. He had come here for peace and quiet, not conversation. But there was no-one in sight.

Tired, he lay down again and tried to dream. He wanted dreams of a rose-covered cottage, sheltered by rolling hills and woods; tranquillity, certainty, contentment. He dreamed of lighting the fire, tending the garden; simple daily tasks, uncluttered by thoughts of why. Dreams of a simple man with simple needs, rising above desire. The world was there – let it be.

"Please listen", said the stone. The philosopher stiffened; then he closed his mind to the intrusion. He sought dreams, not voices: dreams of a simple life untrammelled with the liability of an ever-questing mind. Freedom from the tyranny of curiosity. Peace from the endless battlefield of ideas raging in his brain.

The philosopher was tired; weary of the struggle for knowledge that he suspected might be so simple he failed to see it for looking. Knowledge that might even be there for all to know on passing over. From the vantage point of the next life he would surely understand this one. There were times when it seemed intelligence was a curse, not a boon.

"Excuse me," said the stone. "I know I'm just a simple stone, embedded in the soil of the earth; a drab, round grey thing of no account to anyone, and you are a great and wise philosopher, but I would like to speak with you, if you can spare me a few minutes of your precious time."

The old man sat bolt upright and his dream vanished.

He turned and faced the stone.

"Did you just speak?" he asked in amazement.

"I did," said the stone. "I have been listening to your thoughts, that your brain produces. I don't have a brain that can produce thoughts like that. All I do all day is sit in the soil, and I get very bored. I would like to have a brain like yours so I can think thoughts instead of just sitting in the soil. You are a wise and intelligent man, so perhaps you can tell me how I can get myself a brain like yours. I would so much like to have a brain."

The philosopher had never talked to a stone before, so he was rather taken aback. In fact, he had never realised that stones could talk. But why not? One didn't require a mouth in order to create vibrations in the air. It had seemed to him at times that his oak tree had talked to him, so why not this stone? But a stone wanting a brain?

"It seems to me," said the philosopher, a trifle more pompously than he had intended, "that you are not fully aware of the problems a brain can bring to its owner."

"Quite right," said the stone. "Nor the joys, nor the knowledge, nor the ideas, the excitement of searching, analysing, finding solutions: the sense of power to be had from intelligence. I know none of these things because I don't have a brain. But I would like to know them, so I would like to have a brain. Will you help me to get a brain?"

The philosopher wasn't quite sure what to say.

"I'm not quite sure what to say," he said. "It is something of a responsibility, I would feel, giving a stone a brain, even if I knew how to. I'm not altogether certain it would be wise. In my experience a brain is a very mixed blessing. What if you found it unpleasant? How would you get rid of it? Could you get rid of it? I don't know," he said, shaking his head, "it would worry me."

"There's no need for you to feel responsible," said the stone eagerly. "It is I who want the brain. I won't want to get rid of it. It is all very well for you, you have a brain already. Do you want to get rid of yours?"

"Well, no," said the philosopher, suddenly unsure of his ground. "But I'm a man. I'm supposed to have a brain. That is the natural order of things. It can't be natural for a stone to have a brain, can it?"

The stone sounded a little indignant. "How do you know?" it said. "What do you know about stones? How can you know what it feels like to be a stone without a brain? I think you are just being selfish. You want to keep all the intelligence for yourself." If stones could pout, the stone would have done so.

The philosopher sensed it anyway. The stone's argument had a certain logic to it. What, indeed, did he know about stones? Precious little; if anything. Perhaps stones were supposed to have brains. Perhaps they all had brains except this one, and he would deny it. Or maybe he was destined to put the first brain into a stone. Would stones then take over the world?

The problems posed here were endless. He longed for his little cottage in the fold of the hills. Honeysuckle, he decided, would be nice, and a small lawn. A little stream nearby? Skylarks singing way above the tranquil fields and rooks cawing peacefully atop tall trees.

He did not want to make this decision.

The Philosopher's Stone

"Well?" said the stone impatiently. "Are you going to give me a brain or aren't you?"

The philosopher dithered. All his instincts warned against it, and logic battled with instinct in his brain. Yes, he had a brain. So who was he to deny one to this stone?

He was still dithering when a new voice broke in from behind him.

"Are you talking to that stone?" it said.

The philosopher whirled round, to confront a strange man in a long dark cloak.

"Who are you?" he asked, somewhat nonplussed at this rather untimely arrival. He suddenly felt a little foolish. Perhaps he had been imagining this conversation with the stone.

"I'm a magician," said the man, "and I'm quite certain I heard you talking to that stone."

"I was," replied the philosopher. "It wants me to give it a brain."

"A brain ..." mused the magician. Then he laughed.

"A stone with a brain, eh? Well, well." He crouched down on his haunches and addressed the stone: "So you want a brain, do you?" He chuckled. The philosopher failed to see the joke, but was relieved to have the stone off his hands. For the moment, anyway. He stood back and listened.

"Yes," said the stone, straight to the point. "Can you give me one?"

"I can give you a brain," said the magician magnanimously, "but you will have to pay for it."

"Oh," said the stone, crestfallen. "But I don't have any money."

The Fifth Gift

"You don't pay for a brain with money," said the magician. The philosopher thought that sounded rather ominous, but he kept his counsel.

"What with, then?" asked the stone.

"Well ..." the magician drawled. "If I give you a brain right now, I will return in seven years' time for the payment. By then your brain will have shown you what it is." The philosopher felt a cold shiver run up his back, like icy fingers. He did not like the sound of this at all. He stepped forward.

"I think you will be making a big mistake," he said to the stone. "I know everything has its price, but I don't like the sound of this one."

"Nonsense," said the stone testily. "I want a brain and I don't mind paying for it." It addressed the magician: "Give me a brain right now and I will pay you when you return."

The magician smiled thinly and turned away. Producing a long black stick from beneath his coat, he bent and scratched a peculiar, geometric shape in the soil. Then he stood inside it and turned slowly anticlockwise three times, muttering very softly to himself. He stopped, facing the stone, and put a hand under his cloak. Remaining within the diagram he had drawn, he leaned forward, sprinkled some powder over the stone, then tapped it twice with his stick. With the stick touching the stone for the third time, he closed his eyes and mumbled an interminable, foreign-sounding incantation. There followed a long pause, after which the magician opened his eyes, put the stick away under his cloak, and stepped out of the circle.

Rather negligently he told the stone: "You now have a brain. I will return seven years from today for the payment."

The Philosopher's Stone

He drew his cloak about him, clearly ready to depart.

"But wait," the stone shouted. "I don't feel any different. Where's my brain?" It sounded distraught.

"Your brain," said the magician coldly, "is like a child. It has just been born. It will grow. I will return in seven years' time for my dues."

There was a rushing noise and a wisp of yellowish smoke, then there was no magician any more. The clearing was empty, but for the stone and the philosopher. He wondered if he had dreamt it all, but the sudden harsh voice of the stone confirmed things.

"Well," the voice grated triumphantly, "no thanks to you, but I now have a brain. Soon it will grow and I will have great intelligence. Think of the power it will give me, over all the birds and the animals, and the flowers and trees. They will obey my commands; I will rule over all." The stone actually shook in the ground. "Power," it rambled on, "intelligence and power. All mine, now that I have got a brain."

The philosopher interrupted: "You still must pay for it, and I fear you will pay dearly. But despite my misgivings, and I have many, I will try to help you. In seven years less a day I will return to discover the price the magician demands, and if it is in my power to do so, I will try to assist you. In the meantime, endeavour to use your intelligence wisely." He turned on his heel and walked sadly home, for he felt little hope that the stone would.

True to his word, seven years later less the day, the philosopher returned to the little clearing in the wood where he had met the stone. He had thought much in the intervening years about this day, searched and pondered on the possibilities of what the magician's price might be, but no clear answer had emerged. He approached the meeting with some trepidation.

On the question of stones having brains, he had decided that quite clearly they shouldn't. A brain wasn't a possession like a house, or a pair of shoes. It was more like having a child — it was a responsibility. This particular stone, certainly, did not have the maturity, the sense of values necessary to cope with the responsibility of having a brain. It worried him a great deal.

The stone was still in the same place where he remembered it, looking a little more worn perhaps, but then it was seven years since he had seen it. He suspected that he probably looked a little worn himself.

He walked up to the stone and spoke without preamble: "Well, do you know what the price is?"

The stone seemed to suddenly jolt out of a private reverie. "Yes," it cried, excitedly. "I do. Thank God you have come." And the philosopher felt tentacles like fingers of fire reaching into his brain. His head seemed to implode and he fell to his knees, clutching his throbbing temples, screaming with pain as the stone inexorably sucked from his brain all the knowledge and experience, every thought and solitary idea, feeling, supposition and conclusion that nearly eighty years of philosophical study and reflection had gathered together.

He fell to the ground, spent. The stone seemed almost to swell visibly with all its sudden accumulation of the philosopher's painstakingly acquired knowledge. It didn't speak.

After a surprisingly short while the philosopher rose to his feet. Drained of all that his brain had stored over the years, he stumbled away through the woods, like a child.

The next day the magician arrived, appearing suddenly in front of the stone.

"Well," he said abruptly, "where is it?"

"It's all right in here," gloated the stone just before it shattered into a myriad tiny shards, spreading like motes of dust through the dappled sunbeams filtering down from between the branches of the old oak trees.

The magician walked slowly away, a little smile playing on his lips. It was funny, he mused, how a stone could drain a man's brain, and a man could drain a stone's brain, but a man couldn't drain a man's brain.

~ ~ ~

If he had been a philosopher,

he might have wondered about that.

The young boy closed the book on the
Fifth Gift

and remained a while with his thoughts

in the lonely tower
at the end of the beach

And the Angel watched over him

Get Thee Behind Me

IT WAS late in the evening when the boy finally went in search of the Angel. He had spent a long time struggling with this fifth story. Intelligence? Knowledge? But something did not quite fit. He felt there was something missing; as though the story were incomplete. The magician appeared to have triumphed, which did not seem right; and yet there was a clear hint at the end that he had not. The magician had obviously overlooked something; and that something would seem to be the clue. The boy had clearly missed it as well.

He found the Angel in her cottage, snug beside a cosy fire; for it was a cold night. The boy was glad to join her and he drew up a chair into the warm glow thrown out by the crackling logs. The Angel made tea for them both.

"There is something missing in that story," he said, when he had warmed up. He sat crouched over the cheerful fire, clutching his mug of tea in both hands. "Something I missed anyway," he added.

The Angel peered into the flickering, dancing flames, and thought for a moment. "Yes," she agreed, a trifle reluctantly it seemed to the boy. "It is a little inconclusive in a way." She paused, stirring her tea; then seemed to come to a decision. "Would you like to hear the rest of the story - what happened to the magician afterwards?"

"Yes," said the boy, "I would. Presumably he now has in his brain all the knowledge and wisdom that the philosopher accumulated over the years of his life?" It was a question.

"Presumably," the Angel concurred. Her mind seemed far away. She got up and pottered about the cottage - trimming the lamps, stirring the stew, replenishing the wood-basket. Then she made some more tea and sat down to pick up the story:

"The magician went home, convinced, as you say, that he now had all the knowledge and wisdom from the philosopher's brain. And he was a happy man. For he wanted power, and he knew that supreme intelligence and knowledge, such as possessed by the philosopher, would give him that power.

He lived in a strange land, peopled by wizards and warlocks, witches, werewolves and all those who follow the left-hand path of Lucifer. Many of these creatures had great power, derived from pacts negotiated with the Devil; but the magician wanted to rule them all. And he was cunning enough to know that wisdom gained from other than Satan would be peculiarly powerful in this land, free as it would be from the obligations and restrictions with which the Devil controlled the powers of his acolytes. The Devil would brook no competition from mortals.

And so the magician came home, and immediately began to work on a plan that would enable him to control the whole of the land, and stand even against Lucifer himself. He pored over his ancient books of spells and magic; he scoured the forest at the full moon for powerful herbs and plants – digitalis, amanita, the screaming mandrake. He scrawled cabalistic signs over the walls of his house and chanted strange mantras. He mixed potions and spells, consulted with witches and bats, and studied the Tarot cards to find the most decisive moment to strike.

Finally, he was ready. He had the right potion mixed, the finest conjurations prepared, the correct pattern of pentacle designed. The moon was almost full, and his horoscope confirmed the Tarot's indication that he was now at his strongest.

That night he went out shortly before midnight to a particular spot in the forest, where he marked out the specially designed pentacle in the soil with a stick he had carefully prepared, steeped in a broth of chickens' entrails and bats' livers. He stood in the centre of the star, drank his brew, then walked slowly round the inside of the pattern seven times widdershins, chanting the most powerful invocation to the Devil that he had been able to find.

At precisely midnight, in the streaming silver light of the full moon, he held up his arms and called on Lucifer himself to appear. And in the silver-dappled blackness under the trees where the cold light of that full moon picked out slivers and patches of dead leaves carpeting the forest; where all the rustling and whimpers of nocturnal animals had ceased; in the middle of that dead, cold, dark silence, something began to move.

The ground itself began to move, but no leaves rustled. The trees seemed to back away from the five-pointed star in which the magician stood, clearing a path for something. The earth began to rumble. Black clouds fled across the face of the unsmiling moon, as though running from something. And that cold, milky light flickered and danced, faded, then flickered again, picking out the tumbling dead leaves, heaving on the ground as though on the back of a gigantic surfacing mole.

And a patchy mist arose, from the ground and from the sky, to meet in swirling fronds around the head of the magician. He stood firmly in the centre of his pentacle, holding his little black wand to the sky, chanting still, calling for the presence of the mighty Lucifer. There was no wind, but dead leaves and broken twigs whirled around the magician, caught up in that twirling mist. A deep sighing seemed to emanate from the surrounding trees, then suddenly Lucifer himself stood before the magician – a vision so horrific that he flung up his arm to shield his eyes. His eardrums reverberated with the deep sound of the Devil's voice – a sound that seemed to come from and spread into the earth itself.

'Who dares summon the dreaded Lucifer?'

The magician stood rooted to his pentacle, hardly able to move, the presence of his adversary was so overwhelming. His wand shaking like the branches of the nearby trees, he quickly ran over the spell in his mind – the spell that he had calculated would put the Devil under his power. Now, with the confrontation here, he was suddenly not so sure. With the Devil's next words, he was even less sure.

'I demand once again, and only once, to know who dares summon me – Lucifer, Asmodeus, Satan, Prince of Darkness, Guardian of All Evil, King of All This Land.'

The magician stammered nervously.

'I-I-It is I – the magician – who summon thee.' He sprinkled some powder around the edges of his pentacle and made a sign with his wand. It seemed to give him strength to go on.

'It is I, Oh Lucifer, I who am the greatest magician in this land, the most powerful man between all its four corners; I, with power beyond even thee, who both summon and challenge the Prince of Darkness.' And rapidly he muttered his spell.

He was not quite sure what would then happen, but he certainly had not envisaged what did: the Devil laughed.

The trees shook; even the moon seemed to shiver as the Devil laughed. The magician certainly shivered; things did not seem to be going quite according to plan.

'You dare challenge me? Ho-ho-ho!' roared the Devil. Then he stopped laughing, and the magician started shaking.

'You dare challenge me, miserable magician!' The Devil's voice was cold, thin, ghastly. 'Me – the Lord of All Evil. What gives a worm of a magician the power to challenge Satan himself?'

'I-I-I have power and knowledge, wisdom that is denied you. With that I challenge you for the rule of this land.' But it lacked conviction, even to the magician himself.

'Stolen from the philosopher,' said the Devil, and he spat in disgust.

'From the philosopher you have stolen nothing I do not already possess. All knowledge and all intelligence is mine, including that of the philosopher. Only the philosopher's wisdom — that you thought you had taken — can withstand me.

'But you did not take his wisdom. You took everything from his brain, but his wisdom does not lie there; his wisdom lies in his soul. A man does not create thoughts with his brain, O foolish magician, he simply stores them there; he creates thoughts with his mind, and his mind belongs to his soul. Even I cannot take away from a man's soul what the Lord God has put there; even I, the Great Evil One, can do no more than blind a man to the existence of that soul; I cannot separate him from it, nor from the wisdom therein.'

The magician nearly fainted. Only abject terror kept him standing, as it wildly pumped adrenalin through his shattered body. He had made an horrendous mistake; and the Devil never forgave mistakes.

The Devil pressed on relentlessly: 'If you had had the wisdom of the philosopher, you would have known that I cannot be defeated. Only by the power of the Lord God when he so chooses. A mortal is granted the strength to fight me, but he can never defeat me.

'He can resist me, but never bind me; banish me, but never chain me. Only the Lord God will do that, and only when the time comes. I reign a thousand years, and must be allowed to do so; for how can a man know the glory of God without first seeing me?

'With the wisdom of the philosopher you would have understood that, and you would not have challenged me. You would have left me to lie in the darkness, for I claim only those who seek me.

'And you, magician, have summoned me. You I claim as mine.'

The magician crumpled to the ground clutching his head; and the Devil laughed again.

'For so long you evade me, man of magic, and now you are mine. All that you had, all that you sought, all that you stole, all that you are, is mine.' Then the Devil vanished.

The forest returned to normal; except for the magician, who lay slavering on the ground, his wand and pentacle gone. His teeth seemed a little longer than they had been, and tufty black hairs were beginning to sprout from his face and the backs of his hands."

~ ~ ~

The Fifth Gift - Angel

The Angel poked the embers
and refilled her tea.

"WISDOM," she said, "was the Fifth Gift."

The
6th Gift

George and the Weed

After the disappearance of the Snow Queen on her voyage to the strange planet her daughter, the Ice Princess, was crowned Queen in her place. She became the seventh queen to reign over the kingdom, and seemingly the most benign, despite her cold nature.

    The old rigid social mores and restrictions were swept aside; rules relaxed and regulations rescinded. The Queen's subjects were encouraged to express themselves, in the arts, music and fashion, dancing and singing. Money flowed from the royal coffers, jobs were provided for everyone, and no-one went hungry.

The Queen looked after all. Her mighty army of ministers built huge housing and entertainment complexes for the people, roads and railways, dance halls and leisure centres. Every household had a car and television, every man a wife, every child a social worker. The land flowed with milk and honey; even the clouds and the cuckoos were catered for. Only the Queen's gardener, a grumpy old man named George, was unimpressed.

George was not a happy man. He had three lazy sons who did nothing but preen themselves and go dancing. He could never get them to help him in the garden. Which was fair enough, but then they never did anything else either. And perhaps that was fair enough too, for what else was there? Apart from dancing and drinking and fighting in the streets. There were areas in the city, the old man reflected, that seemed no longer subject to law and order.

But then, order was frowned upon these days. It 'stifled the creative instinct' he had heard some buffoon of an intellectual say on television the previous night. Even he, a simple gardener, knew what twaddle that was. He had spent his whole life with plants, watching them grow and procreate. It was obvious to him that order *was* the creative instinct. All natural creation produced order. Any idiot could see that. Yet the greatest brains in the land did not seem able to. Too simple and blatantly obvious for them, he supposed. Their thoughts were like their clothes — fancy, over-complicated and fashionable.

He could see no end to it all. Perhaps that weirdo pop singer should have wrecked the whole city while he was at it.

Then all those pimps and parasites would have to face up to a bit of real nitty-gritty. Even the Queen, plucked from her ivory palace, might be forced to see life as it really was.

Life for George was certainly not what he would have wished for himself. The Queen paid him little; his house leaked; and his wife, a slatternly woman who did no more than she had to, was the sort who only stopped nagging in order to voice a genuine grievance. There was little comfort for him there.

The only joy in George's life lay in tending gardens. He loved plants. There was a natural harmony to their lives, a balanced flow of patterns, that he had never found in his. He cherished his plants, talked to them, encouraged them. He was, an extremely good gardener.

But he did not like this new palace garden. There was something wrong, something he could not get to grips with. However tenderly he cared for them, his plants just would not grow properly. They barely managed to stagger out of the soil, and were even then stunted, sickly and threadbare. Leaves would die and fall off for no apparent reason. Vegetables were small and tasteless, while flowers often did not bloom at all. If it had not been for the weeds, he would have known there was something wrong with the soil. He could have treated it, or even changed it.

But the weeds – and they were plants after all – grew like wildfire, with no encouragement from him whatsoever. If the weeds grew, so should the plants. But they did not.

Perhaps he just did not spend enough time with them. He seemed to spend so much of each day chopping out weeds, there was little time left for the flowers and vegetables. The weeds grew everywhere, and the faster he raked them out the faster they seemed to grow.

He tried digging them up. He tried burning them. He tried poisoning them. But they just seemed to pop up again as though nothing had happened.

Finally, in desperation, with his garden looking more like a jungle, he went to seek the advice of the Old Wise Woman who lived in the forest. He had known her for many years, and on past occasions when he had consulted her with problems, she had never been wrong. Devious sometimes; obscure frequently; but never wrong. On the other hand she would not always give advice on the problem proffered. Sometimes she would discuss an entirely different matter, apparently unrelated. He always discovered eventually that the advice given was closer to the real heart of the problem than had been the question asked. At other times she would simply refuse to say anything at all. On these occasions the apparent trouble simply sorted itself out.

George often had the uncomfortable feeling that the old woman knew and understood far more than she ever let on. But whatever else happened, she was always sympathetic, so he went to see her. He told neither the Queen nor his wife, for both disapproved most strongly of Old Wise Women and the like. To his wife she was a witch; to the Queen, a senile old fool.

She had expected him, as she always did. George could never fathom out how she knew when he was coming, but she never failed to. It sometimes seemed that she knew before he did. She gestured him to a chair opposite hers by the fire and poured him out a cup of tea, home-made from various herbs gathered in the forest.

Her little cottage was cosy, but simple. She had no possessions to speak of. She would point to her head when asked what she owned, and the sky when asked what she needed. She spoke little. Her age was anyone's guess.

The two of them sat quietly by the fire supping their tea. The old lady smoked, filling her pipe with the gift of tobacco brought by the gardener. After a while she looked at George and shook her head slowly.

"You can do nothing, old man," she said. He had not asked her anything as yet, but she knew, somehow, why he was there. If she had not had such kind, gentle eyes, it would have been most unnerving. But her deep, grey, gentle eyes spoke of an inner goodness. If she knew something, it was right that she should. As was the way she came about it. George just sat and listened, and the old lady continued:

"There is a lack of harmony in your garden, but there is nothing anyone can do. The garden reflects the city, which is full of sickness. The sickness in the city spreads to your garden, and the flowers do not grow straight and strong. The vegetables are not healthy. The leaves die. Only the weeds prosper, as they do in the city.

"It is a natural cycle, a small part of the overall pattern. Its end will come when it is due. Only time will cure your garden, as only time will cure the city." The old lady leaned back in her chair and drew slowly on her pipe.

George was worried.

"Is there nothing I can do?" he pleaded. "The Queen will surely sack me if the garden does not improve soon, and

I have a wife and three idle sons to feed. I will never get another job after being sacked by the Queen. Have you nothing that will kill the weeds?" he asked.

The old lady seemed to think for a moment. Then, without any trace of arrogance, she said simply: "I, of course, can cure your garden, just as I could cure the sickness in the city. But interfering with the natural order of things can produce terrible troubles, far worse perhaps than the ones you have cured. However, I may be able to do something here. You must let me think for a while. It will need to be done very carefully. Come back and see me again tomorrow."

That night George was called before the Snow Queen to explain the state of the garden.

"An absolute disgrace," she had thundered. "I do not pay you inflated wages to grow a field full of weeds. I cannot eat weeds. I cannot decorate my chambers with weeds. What is the good of my paying a gardener to grow weeds? The woods are full of weeds. I do not want them in my garden, do you understand?" The Queen had that delightful habit, so beloved of those in power, of reiterating the obvious; and the paranoic tendency to assume that any error or misfortune is a deliberate plot by underlings to stab her in the back. For underlings it can be very tiresome, and timewasting. The time spent listening to such diatribes can usually be spent more profitably attending to the problem. In this particular case, of course, it could not, but at least George could have been doing something constructive, like watching a quiz show on the television.

George and the Weed

But there was little solace for him at home when his wife found out he was on the verge of losing his job. By the time George reached the old lady's cottage the next afternoon, after yet another browbeating from his sons, he was ready to sell his soul to the devil if it meant ridding his garden of weeds.

Fortunately that did not prove necessary. The old lady had devised a plan.

"Now listen carefully," she said, when he had seated himself and handed over some more tobacco. She gave him a small sack filled with a fine powder. "Sprinkle this over the weeds when you get home," she went on, "and by tomorrow morning they will all have died, except one. That one cannot be killed, and under no circumstances must you attempt to do so. It is there to maintain the continuation of the natural cycle, and thus prevent a complete rupturing of the fabric of events. You are to look after it as you do your flowers – water it and nourish it. Cherish it even, for it will bear tiny white flowers. If it strangles the vegetables nearby, you must allow it to do so. I repeat: under no circumstances must you ever attempt to kill it. If you do, I will not be able to help you. Now go home, but remember what I have told you."

George went home clutching the sack of powder, a very relieved man. An end to the weeds at last, he thought. His job was safe. Perhaps, now, his wife might even stop her incessant complaining. He lived in hopes. He even smiled.

Immediately on arriving at the garden he set to work with the powder, sprinkling it carefully and thoroughly over every single weed. Then he went home, contented and hopeful, and left the powder to do its work.

The next day George was down at the garden early, full of anticipation. And sure enough — he could hardly believe his eyes — it had worked. Not only had the weeds died, but they had disappeared completely. There was not a sign of a weed, dead or alive, anywhere. It was as though a gang of ten men had gone through with hoes during the night, then gathered up the weeds and burnt them. The garden was immaculate.

It was only when he went on a close inspection that he saw it, and remembered the old lady's warning. Right outside the Queen's garden door stood a single weed, on the very edge of the broccoli. It was about two feet tall, with long tendrils spreading across the soil towards the nearest of the vegetables. At the very top of its stem was a delicate crown of tiny white flowers. It was actually quite pretty. George decided he could live with that.

The garden blossomed. George's once-puny vegetables thickened out and grew and grew. His flowers bloomed as never before, filling the air with the fragrance of a thousand scents. And he was never troubled with weeds. Even the slugs and destructive insects seemed to avoid the garden. Only the exquisitely-patterned butterflies flitted around the plants on sunny days, the delicate hues of their fragile wings glinting and flickering in the sunlight. Wild bees purred from flower to flower, picking up and spreading the pollen to fertilise and rejuvenate a garden of which George was now justly proud.

Even the Queen was pleased. Not that she ever stepped into the garden, but the vegetables were the sweetest and finest she had ever tasted, the flowers the admiration of all her visitors. They seemed to fill her chambers with a very special beauty, an indefinable sense of tranquillity. But when she asked George how he had done it, he just smiled and said it was the soil.

Nonetheless, she increased his wages; and even his wife seemed to grumble a little less than usual. They were happy times for George, but he never forgot his promise to the old lady. The weed with the tiny white flowers was treated as well as the rest, and he ignored the fact that the vegetables immediately surrounding it were no better than they had been before. It was a small price to pay. And although he could not understand why one little weed should be so important, he had sufficient faith in the old lady's wisdom to accept the fact.

But one day the Queen did come into the garden. So overwhelmed was she by the quality of the produce and the amazement of her friends, none of whose gardens could produce the like, she decided that she had to see this extraordinary place for herself. She also had the sneaking suspicion that more lay behind the transformation than met the eye. All the gardener would ever say, no matter how much she pressed him, was that the soil was especially good. Why it had suddenly become so good, he would never say. But she was certain he knew. And she wanted to know. She was the Queen, and the people could have no secrets from her. So she arranged a tour of inspection.

She brought with her the Minister of Agriculture (who could produce no theories whatever to explain the sudden and miraculous fertility of this garden), the Minister of Technology (who was quite convinced that some amazing technological discovery was at the root of it), and the Chief of the State Police (who was certain that with a little persuasion the gardener would explain all). And George, clearly very reluctant, showed them around his garden.

Up and down the rows they walked, George pointing out particular items of interest, and trying to sound enthusiastic. The two ministers babbled excitedly, while the Queen simply looked around and made the occasional comment. The Chief of Police followed along behind, watching George carefully. The old gardener could feel those eyes piercing the back of his neck.

But, despite George's forebodings, nothing untoward happened, until they finished the tour outside the back door of the palace. The Queen stopped abruptly, then pointed.

"What is that?" she uttered in a tone of distaste. George's heart sank as his eyes followed the pointing fingers down towards the weed with its crown of tiny white flowers. His brain raced.

"Er ... um ... it's a new type of flower we're trying out, Your Majesty," he stammered, most unconvincingly. The Police Chief's eyebrows shot up in suspicion and he stepped closer.

But the Queen's brain worked on more direct lines.

"Flower?" she snorted. "That's a weed; in my garden. What is that weed doing here, gardener, right outside my back door? I thought you had got rid of them all. You assured me they were all gone." She glared accusingly at poor George, who was not feeling happy at all.

"Er ... we ..ll," he stuttered, "it's only a little one, Your Majesty. And it's not doing any harm tucked away over here."

"Harm?!" the Queen yelled, turning decidedly angry. She waved her arm about her. "Look at those broccoli: dying, all of them. Next thing the whole garden will be overrun again." She turned to George and pointed at the weed. "Get rid of it," she commanded.

George had turned white. "I ... I ... I .... I c-c-can't d-d-do that," he said finally, desperately trying to get the words out. He looked ill.

"Dammit man," the Queen snarled. "What's the matter with you? Do as I say."

George looked as though he was about to faint. He was swaying on his feet, mouth wide open, but he could produce no words. All he could think of was the old lady's warning. She had been very serious, and quite adamant that he never damage the weed. Nothing, but nothing would induce him to so much as touch it. The old lady was not one to jest.

But the Queen was now beside herself with rage, her face suffused with pink blotches. She was not used to being disobeyed. The Minister of Agriculture stepped forward past the white and trembling gardener, and indicated the weed. "Shall I dispose of it, Ma'am?" he offered. "This man," pointing to George, "is clearly not well." He was not an unkind man.

"No," the Queen snarled. "I'll do it myself, like I have to do everything myself around here. Just get that gardener out of the way." She turned to George and almost spat in her fury: "You're fired, you old fool." Then she grabbed a forester's axe that was leaning against the palace wall and chopped the crown of tiny white flowers clean off the stem of the weed. George fainted.

But when he came to nothing had happened. The Queen stood by the decapitated weed, still shaking with anger and still clutching the long-handled axe. Then suddenly, as though it had waited for George, the weed shuddered; and before all their eyes the stem pushed slowly upwards and produced a bud that opened right out into a delicate crown of tiny white flowers. Then it stopped.

George shivered, and looked around him. He could feel menace in the air. But the others did not. They crowded round the weed and stared in amazement.

"This could revolutionise the whole farming industry," announced the Agriculture Minister. But the Minister of Technology was not listening. He had a strange gleam in his eyes.

"We could take over the world with a plant like that," he breathed. The Chief of Police nodded in agreement, plans already formulating in his fertile brain.

But the Queen in her anger was not thinking at all. She guessed she had missed with her first swing, and so tried again. George watched her. He felt strangely detached, and sensed with an absolute certainty that something incredibly horrible was going to happen. The weed had given them all a chance. This time, he decided as the Queen swung the axe down again, it would run out of patience.

As the heavy axe split the crown of tiny white flowers for a second time the weed seemed to literally explode, growing in all directions at once. But there were no more white flowers. Tendrils, as thick as the gardener's fingers, leapt and writhed, spilling out in bunches to pour across the

George and the Weed

ground like a mountain stream. One struck at the Queen like a bullwhip, gripping her neck and squeezing till her eyes bulged like her breasts. And the weed shot up, now the size of a small oak tree, dripping tendrils that sought the ground and then raced in the direction of the palace walls.

The two ministers stood petrified. Not so the Police Chief, however, who was made of sterner stuff. With a gun in each hand he stood back, blazing away at the maddened, writhing weed. Like a cowboy trying to be an actor, thought George dully. Too much television, that was the trouble. These people had it rammed into their heads so much they no longer had any concept of reality. The macho image: so important, yet so often hiding the exact opposite. But was this reality? he wondered. His mind seemed to float, refusing to relate to what was happening before his eyes.

The weed must have been thirty feet high, its tendrils flowing to the ground like the branches of a weeping willow, then spreading out across the palace walls like ivy, creeping and crawling, rooting into every crevice. He heard the crash of breaking window panes as the weed relentlessly pushed its way inside the palace, then the screaming of the servants.

The Queen had vanished beneath the swirling mass of tendrils and her minions were nowhere to be seen. George stood alone at the bottom of his garden watching the weed, that had once lived there harmlessly with its crown of tiny white flowers, methodically tearing apart the magnificent white palace that the old Queen had spent seven years building. Oblivious to the bricks and chimney pots that fell around him, he wondered what the old lady was thinking. He had let her down, when she had obviously stuck out her neck for him. He hoped she wouldn't suffer. Frankly he felt little concern for the others.

The palace was almost in ruins. Beyond the dust and smoke that arose from the burning rubble he could see the weed's outriders — the furthest tentacles — charging down the hill like galloping great green horses. Rearing and plunging, they strode into the streets of the city, crushing people and tearing down houses. Bulbs flickered and blew as the garish neon lights were ripped to the ground, and the half-naked bodies of dancers, courtesans and princes poured screaming into the streets, to be crushed and mangled by the flying tendrils of the weed.

The weed itself, as thick as a house now, seemed to reach the very base of the clouds. Beneath its spreading mantle of green the sky grew dark, lit by occasional streaks of lightning. And George thought he could hear the rumble of thunder. Curiously, no tendrils had encroached on the garden. His flowers still bloomed, a startling splash of colour amid the surrounding devastation. The reds and yellows, pinks, golds and purples stood proudly, bathed in the strange greenish light that was reflected from the weed. And George himself was untouched.

Still the weed grew. It covered the city now till it resembled a long-wrecked ship left dry by the receding tide. And still it galloped on: through towns and villages, farmyards, stations and seaports, to the furthest extremities of the Snow Queen's kingdom. Here the spreading mass of green was joined by more tendrils, reaching down from the upper branches of the weed, wriggling through the clouds to build a curtain from the sky that surrounded the whole kingdom.

Then, as though its job were now done, the weed died; as quickly as it had grown. The millions upon millions of long, snaking green arms withered from their ends, their life seeming to draw back along them and into the stem of the weed. And the stem itself drew back into the earth, until there was only a small green plant with a delicate crown of tiny white flowers to indicate that anything had happened. But the Snow Queen's kingdom was bare; as though it had been stripped by countless quadrillions of voracious soldier ants. Not a building stood. Not a person lived.

Apart from George, who stood in his garden watching little green plants shoot up through the blackened, scorched remains of the Queen's palace, to sprout delicate crowns of tiny white flowers, then stop. A strange welling of music seemed to expand in the still evening air, sweeping from the tiny white flowers to enfold the garden, and George himself. And soft voices began to sing: lilting, rolling songs that flowed back and forth, into and through one another.

The sound grew, a thousand voices harmonising in sweeping melody and counter-melody, building and building till it filled the air like a fragrance. It seemed to blend with all the flowers in the garden, drawing them in to one world with the weeds and the music and George.

A feeling of intense joy and deep tranquillity suffused the old, tired gardener, spreading warmth and energy through his weary body. He stood straighter, more erect. He felt younger. He felt at peace.

He turned to face the smouldering remains of the old palace, from where the music seemed to come.

As he stood there he saw an arm
thrust out from the ashes and reach upwards,
clutching a battered old thirteen string guitar.

And through the heavenly music

an unmistakable voice

called out :

Here - Comes

My - Band

Again

~ ~ ~

The young boy closed the book on the
Sixth Gift

and remained a while with his thoughts

in the lonely tower
at the end of the beach

And the Angel watched over him

The Neverending Story

THE BOY laughed. "He didn't wreck the place again, did he?"

"Of course not!" The Angel was short.

The boy stopped laughing, and said seriously: "I think this one must be Eternal Life - new life growing from the ashes of the old. The indestructibility of life. I think this gift is Eternity."

"It is," said the Angel. "The guardian's Sixth Gift was ETERNITY. However people may change and die; however they are destroyed, the essential life that is in them - their spirits - cannot be. The life of a man's spirit is forever."

The boy nodded absently. He seemed unsure.

"I think there is more to the story than just that," he said.

The Angel pondered for a while before replying.

"Perhaps you are right," she conceded. "This gift does have certain strings attached to it, none of which" - she stressed - "affect the basic quality of the gift. Spiritual life is eternal, and that cannot be altered. Its progression can, though."

The Angel paused, gathering her thoughts.

"Do you remember the salmon?" she asked him.

"Yes."

"And how horrified you were at the prospect of them never reaching their goal?"

"I do," he said with some feeling.

"Well; Eternity," she elaborated, "can be viewed as a series of goals - an infinite progression of spawning grounds, with rest and recovery here between each. It is countless lives and deaths - incarnation and return - each different, each containing something for us to do - something for us to learn.

"Eternity is a never-ending cycle of cycles; and although the Eternal Cycle can never be ended, it can be frozen. It is possible to become trapped in one particular cycle for an indefinite period."

"Wow!" The boy's eyes were wide. "You mean like a salmon that can never reach the spawning grounds?"

"Something like that. We must learn the lessons of each cycle before we can pass onto the next. Just as you have had to learn the secret of each of these books before you could read the next.

"If we do not learn the lessons, we have to go through that cycle again and again until we do. As you would have to read the book over and over until you understood it."

"Wow!" the boy muttered again. "I don't like the sound of that. Does it happen often? Are the lessons very difficult to learn?" He looked worried, perhaps thinking of his own coming lifetime.

The Angel shook her head encouragingly. "No," she said, "the lessons are not difficult to learn. But there are distractions, as you saw in the story of the fifth gift. The learning does require perseverance and a strong will. When these are lacking, it is possible to get caught in a recurring cycle. And the longer one remains in the same cycle, the more difficult it becomes to get out of it.

"Added to which, there are no rest periods, as there are between changing cycles."

The boy whistled. "So the destruction of the Snow Queen's palace, yet again, was a sign of her kingdom being caught up in a recurring cycle?"

"That's right."

"Because of the behaviour of the Queen and her subjects?"

The Angel smiled wryly. "Well, they did not learn much from their lives, did they? Hardly on a par with the philosopher and the bosun, or George for that matter. Or even Coalhole Custer.

"These four all learnt what their lives showed them. And by varying means were released from the recurring cycle that gripped the kingdom.

"The bosun's sensitivity to his experiences drove him back to his island and away from the trapped kingdom. The philosopher's enforced childhood preserved him automatically from reentering the cycle, while George was simply left alone by the weed because it knew he had cared for it. Coalhole Custer was literally blown out of the cycle by the power and honesty of his music."

There was a pause. "But what about Henry? The honey bee? Surely he learnt his lesson?"

A smile spread slowly across the Angel's face at the

The Sixth Gift - Angel

memory of Henry the honey bee, and she took her time answering the boy's question. Finally she said rather enigmatically: "When you have read about the seventh gift you will understand the deeper significance of Henry's experiences, and also those of the old lady dying in hospital."

The boy thought for a moment about all this before he spoke again.

"Well, then presumably the Snow Queen and her kingdom will start life all over again, just as it was before?"

"Yes," said the Angel. "And live it as they did before. And they will go on doing so until they learn what their lives are trying to show them. Only then will they be able to break their bonds and enter a fresh cycle."

"Mmm..." The boy was pensive. "That's some penance," he said. "But...... I still don't quite see how Coalhole Custer fits into all this. I mean, he seemed to be appearing in the recurrence of the cycle. Yet you say he escaped it."

"He did," the Angel confirmed. "Although he appeared as the Snow Queen's cycle began yet again, he was, himself, in a new one. Coalhole Custer, you will discover, is not a part of the Snow Queen's kingdom, so he cannot be trapped in its cycles."

~ ~ ~

The Neverending Story

The Seventh Gift

The Beauty

Of the Beast

Quite what Coalhole Custer's guitar and left arm were doing poking out of the smouldering ashes of the Snow Queen's palace, we may never know. A more enquiring mind than George's might have hung around to see what would happen. George, however, had had enough.

So far as he could tell, there was not a living soul left in the land - not a person nor a thing, save only his garden.

Perhaps the weeds would take care of that; or maybe that bearded weirdo of a pop singer — if that really was him under the ashes — could do it. For George had no intention of staying around himself.

He took one last long look at the garden, a blaze of colour and cheer amidst the desolate, smoking landscape. It was a nice garden, he thought; who would have believed it could cause so much trouble. He hoped it would be alright without him. He experienced a slight twinge of conscience at leaving it; and almost began to feel that he could be persuaded to stay.

But a sudden rumbling noise from the ashes of the palace persuaded him otherwise. George turned and fled, just as a strange-looking object, that a musician would have recognised as a psychological synthesiser, pushed its ungainly way into the thick, dust-laden daylight. If Coalhole Custer's band really was coming back, George did not want to see it.

The old gardener did not stop running until he reached the coast, where he shipped aboard the first vessel he saw that was bound for foreign lands.

"Anywhere!" he panted, when the Master asked him where he was headed. "Fine," said the Master. "That's where we are going."

So the old man of the land took to the sea. And the clean salt air slowly healed the wounds in his heart, and cleansed his soul of the hurt and hate and anger seared into it by the things he had seen.

More there may have been to what he had seen than the old man saw. But he was a simple soul, and saw only through his eyes.

Later that night, feeling a little calmer, he stood on the bridge with the Master as the old steamship Malachi Jones rolled and rattled her way slowly south, searching for a peaceful harbour far from the ravaged ruins of the Snow Queen's realm. It was a wild, black night, unrelieved by stars or moon. The ship, weary from too many years plodding the seas, wallowed badly, lurching into the waves and shattering them into gleaming sheets of spray that hammered on the bridge windows.

The Master, tall and thin, taciturn at the best of times, was gloomy.

"There's evil about," he muttered to George through the pipe he had clenched tightly between his teeth. "I can smell it in the air."

George shuddered. He had come to sea to get away from that sort of thing.

The Master looked at him sideways. "That weed's not following you, is it?" He spoke tentatively.

George laughed nervously, and glanced over his shoulder. "Don't be ridiculous," he said. But he felt uneasy. He shook his head to try and banish the thoughts that now welled up in his brain. The weed had left him alone. Why should it follow him now? All the same, he peered round in the darkness, the hairs crawling on the back of his neck.

"I don't like it," said the Master. And at that moment the two of them were rooted by a long, drawn-out, almost bestial scream from somewhere on the poopdeck. As one they whipped round and stared through the after bridge window into the darkness.

But around the stern of the ship it was no longer dark.

The Seventh Gift

A strange green light lit up the whole of the poop, and the two men could see a sailor there, crouched on his knees with his hands over his head. Towering above him, and way above the after cargo mast, swaying at the end of a long reptilian neck was a head. Perhaps twice the size of the wheelhouse and oval-shaped like that of a serpent, it glowed bright green, pulsating around a single eye that blazed with the ferocity of a red-hot coal. Above the eye, and clearly visible in the green light that shone around the beast's head, rested a crown of tiny flowers, each one as black as the surrounding night.

George fainted.

The Master stared for what seemed a very long moment, then leapt to the engine room voice-pipe. He wrenched out the bung and yelled down to the engineer: "Full speed, Jimmy! Everything you've got. There's a bloody monster up here; sea serpent or kraken or something. For God's sake give her the gun!"

He looked back astern over his shoulder, but the beast had not moved. It just hung its great head about fifty feet above the ship, and seemed to watch them. The Master began to shake, then he ran to the wheel and bellowed into a microphone.

"All hands to the bridge. Emergency Stations. Emergency Stations. All hands to the bridge. Bosun – break out the small arms; report to the Master."

The old Malachi Jones strained and heaved and shook as the engineer stoked up his boilers for all the speed he could get. And sailors appeared from all over the ship, running for the bridge with rifles and shotguns.

Then another glowing head appeared, on the port side of the ship. It was identical to the first, even to the crown of tiny black flowers. And another appeared on the starboard side, then two more.

By the time all hands were gathered in the wheelhouse the ship was surrounded by a circle of seven huge green heads, all identical, all with crowns of tiny black flowers. And each one just swayed way up above the ship, staring down as though bemused by what it saw. Or perhaps still looking for what it sought.

None of the heads made any sound, and all seemed to sway in unison, as though they belonged to one single monstrous creature.

Heaven preserve us, thought the Master; it must be ten times the size of the ship. If it attacked them, they were all dead. What was it doing?

For fully half an hour it did nothing, except keep station with the Malachi Jones and peer down on her, with all its seven heads. The ship was bathed completely in the eerie green light, and the sailors clustered terrified in the wheelhouse, clutching their clearly inadequate weapons.

What in heaven's name is it waiting for? the Master wondered. Then George came to. Still groggy, and with no recollection of why he had fainted, he stood up. And the nearest head jabbed viciously at the wheelhouse.

There was a rending crash as wood and glass shattered and splintered, and screams came from the sailors diving for cover. A long slimy tongue, forked at the end like a snake's, licked out and curled round George's body. Then its head came down, and the great eye, blazing like a furnace, peered into the wheelhouse as though inspecting the old gardener.

It hung for a moment. And the Master seized his chance. He grabbed a large rocket flare, aimed it straight into the eye, and yanked the firing pin.

There was a shattering explosion and a shower of sparks filled the wheelhouse. The beast's head jerked up with a bellow that blew the remnants of the wheelhouse roof right out into the sea; and it dropped George.

My God, thought the Master, it's after the old man. He looked round frantically. George was sprawled in a corner clutching his head, and the Master could see another tongue snaking out towards him.

In one bound he was across the bridge. He grabbed George by the shoulders and practically threw him down the companionway to the radio shack.

"Lock him up!" he yelled at the petrified radio operator.

George fell to his knees on the floor of the tiny, steel-clad room. As seven reptilian heads crashed into the broken wheelhouse in a desperate bid to seek him out, he put his hands together and prayed with all his heart and soul to the Old Wise Woman to deliver them from this evil.

Amidst all the panic and screams, and the crash of firearms and flares, no-one noticed the dense cloud suddenly break apart over to the south-west. It revealed a round glistening full moon, that threw a path of light across the sea towards the troubled ship. In the light, racing towards them was a dolphin: a pure white dolphin that shone like a leaping halo as it bounded down the streaming silver pathway of moonlight.

The Master was the first to see it, clambering to his

feet as the beast withdrew its heads on failing to find George. Why don't I just throw him overboard? he was thinking, then perhaps this damned thing will leave us alone.

Then he saw the white dolphin. The Master of the Malachi Jones, like most experienced seamen, had grown up with the legend of the white dolphin, which was reputed to appear at times when a ship was in great distress, and then guide it to safety. The Master knew nothing of the origins of this tale, nor the reasons for the dolphin's rumoured behaviour, but deep in the recesses of his mind the ancient race memory of his breed awoke at the familiar sight of the dolphin surging through dark seas towards a stricken ship. If the Master could have tuned in to this memory he would have seen the very first stirrings of the legend begin to form.

He would have seen circling way above a small, lonely white dolphin a Fairy Tern, which was a small white bird, rather delicate in appearance with long pointed wings, to whom everything was possible and all things had meaning. She had been following the solitary white dolphin for some days now as he ploughed his lonely way through the cold southern seas, and she listened to his thoughts — the ones he understood; and also the ones he did not.

They were strange thoughts for a dolphin: thoughts that had so perturbed his peers they had cast him out of the school to wander the seas alone, disturbing the balance of only himself.

And so he roamed, sensing somewhere a solution to the troubles that seemed to be all his thoughts brought him; searching endlessly within himself and without for the tiniest clue as to where those thoughts might lead.

The more he searched the more he learnt; and the less he seemed to understand. As each piece clicked into place in the puzzle, so the final picture seemed to recede a little further, into the depths where perhaps a dolphin's thoughts should not go.

His confusion turned gradually to bewilderment: then despair; and finally fear as the conflicting images whirled into a crescendo of doubts that the little dolphin's brain seemed incapable of containing.

Yet he clung still, to the train of thought that he knew must ultimately lead him from the dark tunnel into light. And as he struggled with the demons that would hold him in the darkness, the depth, intensity and sincerity of his anguish drew to him the Fairy Tern.

For six days and six nights she followed the stricken young dolphin but did nothing, save perhaps test his resolve. And on the seventh day, although he was never to know it, he was no longer alone.

But he sensed something: an easing of the tension perhaps; a semblance of clarity creeping into his thoughts. There was no great revelation, but for some unaccountable reason he felt calmer. The fog that filled his brain seemed to clear a little, and he began vaguely to see some sort of way ahead.

And what he saw, as the Fairy Tern circled lazily far above him, was a small sailing ship crossing ahead of his path.

In itself, this was of no great import. He had seen ships before and knew they were sailed by men. And he knew something of men, from the tales of his elders — legends and stories of a certain inexplicable relationship that seemed to exist between them and dolphins. No-one knew why or when the relationship had begun, but their history was filled with stories of both creatures working together to catch fish; and also tales of dolphins rescuing men from the sea – which was to them an alien environment.

He had never thought much about this before, but suddenly, now, the whole curious business seemed to fill his head with anomalies and unresolved questions. And as he pondered on this strangeness, he realised that something was niggling at the back of his brain. Something to do with that sailing ship ahead. Where was it going, he wondered?

Idly he checked its course with his sonar. As it registered, he felt his body stiffen, his nerves jangling. Casting aside his musings, he double-checked the course, then carefully probed the waters out ahead of the ship. She was running straight towards a jagged reef close beneath the surface. He had to warn the sailors.

The little white dolphin, all confusion gone, fairly flew through the water towards the endangered ship. He circled it close at great speed, leaping constantly from the water in an attempt to attract attention.

A small knot of sailors soon gathered at the rail to watch the unusual sight of a pure white dolphin cavorting like a mad thing around their ship. They were used to dolphins swimming ahead of them, diving deep in the night to leave glowing tunnels of phosphorescence in the water behind them; interwoven in magic trails of light about the ship's course. They were said by some to bring storms when they leapt high in the daytime, but sailors liked dolphins. They sensed, perhaps, this curious relationship.

However, none of these sailors had ever seen a white dolphin before, nor one that leapt around so wildly as this one, and they stared in fascination, cheering him on.

But when the dolphin began swimming purposefully ahead of the ship, then suddenly turning to starboard, repeating the manoeuvre time and again, an old Able Seaman sensed something amiss and ran for the Captain.

The Captain, who was a very experienced seaman, took one look at the dolphin's antics and ordered the wheel put hard to starboard. He had seen this behaviour before, and knew one fellow master who had wrecked his ship through ignoring it.

The moment the ship altered to a safe course, the dolphin leapt high in the air, landing flat on the water with a colossal splash. Then he swam rapidly back and forth along the ship's new track, porpoising smoothly to indicate to the watching sailors that all was now well.

The Captain waved his thanks to the white dolphin, then returned to the chartroom to check his position; but the other sailors remained at the rail, waving and cheering till the warmth of their feelings flowed right across the water and into the dolphin's now tired body.

The little dolphin felt a glow in his heart that he had not known since he could remember. He felt a joy that he had not believed possible. And he felt a certainty of purpose that he never thought he would find.

Men were adrift on this ocean, in constant danger from rocks and storms. Alone in a hostile world.

But to the little white dolphin it was home: it was his world and he knew and understood it. It was for him to guide these men to safety. That was the tradition. That, surely, was his purpose.

Way above him, with needle-sharp eyes, the Fairy Tern floated on the wind currents, her long narrow wings still, curved to the flow of the air. And still she stayed with him.

Through all the following days and nights, as the white dolphin patrolled the seas in search of ships in danger, the Fairy Tern remained overhead. Unseen and unknown she continued to accompany him; as though her task were not yet done.

And this day she watched as the little white dolphin sped through the waves towards the stricken and wallowing Malachi Jones. The Master of the Malachi Jones had always paid lip service to the charming idea of a white dolphin speeding to the rescue in times of trouble, but now that it actually seemed to be happening to him the superstitious side of the old seaman sent an involuntary shiver through his body at the prospect of yet more inexplicable events.

He stared numbly out of the bridge window, wondering what on earth a little white dolphin could possibly do to save them from the horror that hung still over his poopdeck. Then he saw Pilot Jack – for that was the name sailors had given him – leap skywards ahead of the ship in a cloud of roiling phosphorescence, then plunge back in the water and swim away in the direction of the land away on his port side.

"He wants us to follow him," said the Mate in awed tones from the other side of the bridge.

"Well we can't go in there," the Master barked. "This coast is riddled with uncharted rocks and sandbanks. We wouldn't get half a mile without piling up on something."

"That's as maybe," muttered the Mate through nervous clenched teeth that had already bitten halfway through the stem of his pipe. "But how long are we going to last out here?" His point seemed to be stressed by the great leering red eye that suddenly fell from the sky and stared directly into the face of the Master.

"Oh my God!" growled the Master. "Pass me the binoculars, quick!" Then, trying to ignore the horrendous eye that glowered no more than ten feet from his head, he focused the glasses on the dim white shape of the speeding dolphin.

And his heart leapt in sudden hope as he saw the dolphin weaving and jinking as he went, where before he had been swimming straight.

"Bloody hell," he muttered. Then he yelled: "The dolphin's following a channel, I swear it. He's showing us the way through the rocks. If we can get in there surely this damn thing won't be able to follow us." He turned to the Mate. "Take the wheel, mister, and follow that dolphin!"

The old Malachi Jones staggered over the next wave then almost rolled her funnel into the back of it as the Mate wound the wheel hard over to port in an effort to get her round before the next wave should catch her beam on. The tired old engine shrieked in protest as the prop came out of the water and raced in thin air, then suddenly she was on course astern of the dolphin. The seas were on her quarter now and she rolled heavy and uneven, like a drunk falling out of a pub. But she was headed for dangerous waters, and all aboard prayed that the beast would not be able to follow. They also prayed that the white dolphin really was guiding them through the safe channel.

Half a mile ahead of the ship there stood a white wall of boiling, breaking water where the waves piled up and broke against the hidden rocks and banks. Neither the Master nor the Mate could see a way through, and the latter's knuckles were white against the dark, battered varnish on the spokes of the wheel. The Master called the Bosun to take the other side of the big wheel to help the Mate. Even if there was an entrance through that breaking water, it would be a battle to get the ship through. The old bucket did not handle very well at the best of times, being fat and weed-strewn, with an engine that chuffed most of its power out of the funnel.

But as the ship was almost into the breakers the Master saw Pilot Jack suddenly turn hard to port and disappear round the back of a huge standing wave whose crest was continually breaking higher than the bridge.

"Get after him!" he yelled at the Mate, who was already hauling on the wheel. The Master leapt forward and put his back beneath a spoke and heaved in unison with the other two. The Malachi Jones shuddered round slowly, too slowly as the Master could see all too clearly, and the great white wave loomed up over the bridge like a sheer rock face. Then, as she hung athwart the face of the following wave, it suddenly broke and flung the ship bodily sideways past the white monster.

"Hard-a-starboard!" yelled the Master in desperation as he spotted a slick of flat water right behind the standing wave, in which the white dolphin lay as though waiting for them. The Malachi Jones rolled violently to port, dipping her bridge window right into the wave that now rolled under them, then she seemed to just ping through the gap like a flicked coin.

"Hold her steady, mister," came the cry from the Master, as he saw Pilot Jack bound off ahead into the mess of rocks, shoals and white water that lay between them and the shore. They were committed now; there was no hope of turning back and finding their way out. He did not even know what lay over on the shore; could only hope and pray that there was a safe haven and that the dolphin would lead them into it. He stared out of the bridge window, an arm firmly wrapped round the compass to steady him against the vicious rolling and lurching that the steep, high seas were causing in his ship. The night was black and the waves were white, and it was a seaman's nightmare.

As they staggered and lurched their way deeper into these wild, breaking seas in pursuit of the white dolphin, the Master gradually became aware that he had not seen any large red eyes for a while. He looked astern of the ship and there was no sign of the monster. He picked up the binoculars and scanned the sea astern of them, and finally saw a dim green glow way in the distance.

"We've lost the beast!" he cried out. "Left him out in the deep water. Thank God!" He pulled the bung out of the radio room voice-pipe and shouted down: "You can come up now! The beast has gone." And a moment or two later the radioman came up onto the bridge with old George.

"How are you feeling?" the Master asked him.

George shook his head groggily. "Alright. I'm alright." Then he looked around. "What's happened?"

The Master told him what had been going on, then pointed ahead to Pilot Jack, who was swimming steadily no more than twenty yards from the ship. "... and there he is," he finished off, in hushed tones such as one might use when speaking in a church.

George looked stunned, clinging grimly onto the Master's chair and staring out at the white dolphin. Then he stared at the white water and the broken irregular seas that crashed into the ship from all directions. Then he stared back out to sea, to where the Master had said the beast was. George was petrified, but he was not sure what of; there seemed to be so much around him that he should be terrified of and the old man could not cope with it all. Finally he gave up thinking about any of it and simply clung vacantly to the chair – it seemed the only secure and solid thing in his life at that moment.

The Master meanwhile was inspecting the approaching shoreline through his binoculars, and it looked wild in the steadily worsening weather. He could see huge clouds of spray hung along the cliffs like rain as, in the gradually dawning twilight, the waves rolled in, foaming white across the rocks, to explode in cascading sheets against the sheer face of the cliffs. He could see no sign of harbour or shelter in the direction the dolphin was taking them. Yet somehow he felt untroubled; perhaps it was because of the certain knowledge that he now had no choice but to follow their self-appointed pilot.

The cliffs grew ever larger – and George ever more frightened – as the old ship wallowed her way ever closer to that forbidding shore, a welter of black, jagged rocks and

The Seventh Gift

flying white spume. And still no sign of a gap.

Pilot Jack had fallen back a little until he was just visible under the plunging bows of the Malachi Jones. How he avoided that lethal stem as it reared up on the waves and crashed into the troughs, twisting its way towards the breakers, George had no idea.

Suddenly the little dolphin accelerated away from the ship, leaping ever higher, and vanished round the back of the nearest razor-edged rock pinnacle. A moment later he reappeared and resumed his station close ahead of the ship. He repeated this manoeuvre twice, as though to make sure he had been seen. His speed must have been phenomenal for he seemed to be away barely a moment, although it felt like a lifetime to George.

The Master tapped the old man on the shoulder and pointed to the narrow gap.

"There's our haven," he said. "Behind there somewhere." He reached over and rang the engine room telegraph to slow speed ahead, so as to give him some power in reserve for any rapid manoeuvring that might be needed. The Master's caution had been sharpened by a lifetime at sea.

The dolphin remained close ahead of them as he piloted the ship so close to the pinnacle that George could almost have reached out and touched it. The water boiled through the gap and around the rocks, and the Master put two men on the wheel again to keep the ship running straight.

As they rounded the rock, George nearly fainted again. He had been expecting calm waters – a wide, land-locked and sheltered harbour. But all he could see were more rocks, more breakers, more cliffs. Even the Master began to worry as he felt a strong surge sucking his ship uncontrollably towards a tiny steep beach between the cliffs, upon which the surf pounded like a steam hammer.

In the broadening daylight he could see on the beach a small group of men, gathered round a signal fire. They were waving wildly at the ship, beckoning it towards the beach.

"Look!" cried George. "There must be shelter there somewhere. We're saved!" He turned to look at the Master, relief flooding through his old body like a tide.

But the Master stood white-faced at his side, one eye on the men at the fire ahead of them and one on the white dolphin, who was leaping wildly from the water and racing away on their starboard side towards the mouth of a huge cave in the rock face.

The old seaman's brain was whirling. They could not both be right – the men on the beach calling him one way and the dolphin leading him another. In that tight, rock-strewn hole he had perhaps three seconds in which to make a decision, before he wrecked his ship with all hands.

He glanced at the beach. Rescuers? Or Wreckers? These had been rife along the Snow Queen's coast. But he had never heard of a dolphin leading a ship into danger. He made his decision.

He leaned over the bridge wing and yelled down to the fo'c'sle hands to let go the starboard anchor at short stay, ordered the wheel put hard a-starboard and the engine to full ahead. All more or less in the one breath. Then he gripped the front of the bridge wing and watched.

As the anchor took hold in the seabed, a huge curling wave picked up their stern and carried it forward. The ship lurched hard round to starboard virtually on the spot, the anchor holding the bow while engine and wave combined to drive the stern round and past it. Then the stern sank into the following trough, down and down until it hit the bottom with a sickening, grinding crunch. George felt the whole ship shudder and rattle. Then she bounced clear, and with the engine screaming at full speed the little ship began struggling forward, now pointing towards the cave entrance.

The anchor was hove in rapidly and the engine slowed again, and the Master, streams of perspiration running down his face, conned his ship in towards the cave, close behind the dolphin.

George, white and trembling in every nerve, clung terrified to the rail as the Malachi Jones bore in towards the black hole ahead of them, yawing wildly almost beam on to the face of the next approaching and breaking wave. The Master frantically ordered full port wheel to try and hold her straight, then everything went black as they vanished into the hole in a welter of white water.

It seemed only a moment later that they rocketed out into a vast, sheltered, tree-lined lagoon. The wave rolled in harmlessly behind them, all its violence broken by the walls of the tunnel. George wept with relief as the Master quietly rang down for dead slow ahead, then he gripped the rail firmly to try and stop his hands shaking. Ahead of them Pilot Jack swam slowly towards a small cluster of houses on the north shore, and a short while later the Malachi Jones lay safely and peacefully at anchor. The dolphin lay alongside the ship, breathing heavily and rolling a little in the slight swell that was all that remained of the seas they had come through.

And there they remained. The natives were friendly, there was plenty of food and water ashore, and there was nowhere else to go. Above them, unseen, the Fairy Tern circled, watching her dolphin as each day he went out to sea to seek out and bring in more straggling ships from the very jaws of the beast.

"He asks for nothing," the Master said to George one day some weeks later, "and gives everything. What drives him, I wonder? What do you suppose goes on in that head of his?"

No-one knew. But the sailors aboard the many ships that now lay anchored safely around the lagoon cared for and cherished their dolphin. Nets were cast in the shallow bays for the fish that Pilot Jack would drive towards them, and the men always made sure the dolphin got his share. There was little else they could do for him as he seemed to need nothing; only, perhaps, their companionship. But the warmth of their feelings for him spread into their feelings for one another, so what they could not give him they shared amongst themselves. It was a happy little community. And a lonely, wandering dolphin seemed at last to have found himself a purpose.

Yet the Fairy Tern remained.

As did the wreckers. And they did not share the sailors' love for the dolphin that deprived them of so much business.

One dark night, late while the sailors slept, they rowed out stealthily into the lagoon and netted the dolphin. They dragged him to shore and hung him up on a tree by the water's edge to die of dehydration, and from the cuts and gashes and bruises where they had beaten him almost senseless in their rage.

George and the Master found him early the next evening when they were out collecting fruit. He was dead by then. And their beloved dolphin was no longer white and pure, but torn and battered, smeared with black, congealed blood and crawling with flies. He hung from the tree like rotting carrion.

The two men stood for a moment in stunned silence. Then George went berserk.

"It's the wreckers! The filth, the scum!" He broke down and wept.

Then the old gardener's horror turned to cold anger. "Get me a gun," he snarled at the Master. "Get me a gun!"

The Master, who seemed very calm, gripped his friend's arm tightly. Although his own body trembled from his attempts to hold back the revulsion, and the instinctive desire for retribution that surged through him like a wave, he managed somehow to speak quietly.

"No, George," he said. "No. He would not want that. He loved us all, and he would have saved them from themselves, just as he saved us all from the beast, if they had only let him." His whole body shook from the emotions he was suppressing. "I know how you feel, George, believe me," he almost cried, "but it would be wrong to compound evil with more of the same. Let it be, George. Remember what happened in your garden. There is evil trying to grow here but we must not feed it, we must not let it spread to us. It would wreck everything he did, and everything he stood for."

The Master reached out with his knife and cut down

the body of the white dolphin. Then he turned back to George.

"He's not gone, George. They can destroy his body, but as long as we don't succumb to this evil he will live on in us, and in our children and our children's children; if we hold true to what he has taught us."

He paused, and stared for a long while out over the lagoon, as though a thought had struck him. Then he continued: "You know, George, we're none of us the same people we were."

High above them the Fairy Tern wheeled on her long white wings and left. Her job was done: Pilot Jack had found his purpose. And the Master and George buried him, deep within the roots of a nearby, lonely leafless tree, whose solitude seemed to cry for sustenance.

~ ~ ~

And as the last of the Earth
closed over the white dolphin,
faint wisps of a strange, familiar music
began to swirl around the grave,
like early morning mist
rising through the curiously shaped,
thirsting roots of a tree
destined to be for ever nourished
by the death of this dolphin.

It was not to bring peace

that

the singer came

The young boy walked for a long while
after this final story

away from the lonely tower
and down towards the sea

where there grew a tree

curiously shaped
like a guitar with too many strings

And with him went his thoughts

And beside him walked the Angel

I Come Not To Bring Peace

THE ANGEL watched the young boy trudging wearily along the sand, his hands deep in his pockets and his head bowed low. She saw him stop and talk to some fishermen hauling their nets by the shore.

It seemed unfair, she thought, for one so young to have such responsibility and such loneliness. To be incarcerated yet again in a physical body, isolated from the familiarity of his own world, and faced with a task of this immensity, was beyond what anyone could reasonably expect. Yet he expected it of himself. Accepted it quietly.

He was stronger, she suspected, than anyone knew; more resilient than perhaps even he realised. He would survive this ordeal, as he had the last. And at this attempt she was certain he would succeed in blowing wide open the recurring cycle that gripped his beloved Earth. Particularly as this time he would have a little assistance on her part.

He would find out, of course; and he would remember the stories when he discovered the situation. But it seemed to her that he deserved a little help. He knew as well as she that only through suffering could a man gain true understanding. But surely that applied to the people of Earth no less than it did to him? It was not right, she felt, that he should take on all the suffering himself.

He had to the first time, to make a necessary point. But that point had been made now. If those who lived on the Earth were ever to understand his gifts, it seemed fairly obvious to her what had to be done. And she had exercised her not inconsiderable talents to ensure that it was.

She watched the boy walk away from the water till he found a large rock at the edge of a pool. He sat down on the rock and, with his elbows resting on his knees, he lowered his chin into the palms of his hands and stared out to sea.

There was just one problem, the Angel reflected. Her slight modification to the general run of events on Earth might make it rather difficult for his final, and most precious gift to be accepted. On the other hand, she knew that without her assistance he would have just as much difficulty getting any of the gifts accepted as he had had the last time. Something had to be changed, and someone other than the boy had to change it. He would never have countenanced what she had done if he had known.

Well, no doubt he would sort that problem out. He

I Come Not to Bring Peace

had read the stories; he knew how these things were done. Besides, it would do the people of Earth no harm at all to make a bit of an effort in the aftermath. Hopefully they might have learnt something by then. If they had not, they never would.

She walked slowly down the beach towards the rock upon which the boy still sat, still staring out to sea. She had no doubts that he now knew who he was, and what he had to do. And what his seventh gift was.

The Angel stood quietly behind him for a few moments, alone with her thoughts and her singer; then she closed her eyes and looked deep into her mind, down onto the still-smoking rubble piled high up where the old Snow Queen's palace had once stood.

She watched the rubble slowly erupt in an expanding mushroom of dust and stones as her wild, yellow-haired singer emerged with his band and once more headed across the kingdom, spreading yet again fear and hatred amongst those remaining as he sang new songs drawn from mountains no man had seen. His music raged ahead across the land, a wild, swirling cloud of chords laying waste like locusts to all that was soulless before it. No building, no business, no graven image, no icon, no treasure, no wealth, no monument, no falsehood, no priest, no king, no courtier, no Prince could stand beside this music — only people. People were all that his passing spared; and a great fear was wrought in many on seeing this.

And their fears were fanned by the breath of the dying Beast into a hot and foetid hatred that clamoured for the death of the singer's songs. But the bandmaster could no longer be destroyed, for he marched now with Nellie Matilda at his right hand and Henrietta at his shoulder, and ahead of him went the philosophers, the gardeners and the sailors, to prepare the way.

These disciples built with him a new kingdom that would one day enable the young boy to break the people's bonds, for they worked with tools the others had not possessed.

In the wake of the band the young boy walked alone and calm through the scattered human debris, seeking survivors amongst the emotional wreckage of the Angel's actions. No bitterness accompanied him for he now understood why she had done this thing.

And as he walked, those capable still of seeing such on this sad and lonely Earth saw who he was and reached out, like drowning men, for the gifts he offered. And to each he gave gladly.

Then from the spirits of these few his seven precious gifts spread inexorably, like slow ripples on a pond, into the spirits of their children, and thence their children's children and their children's children's children; until eventually the day came when all the people on Earth were imbued with the spirit and the essence of the young boy's gifts.

And the gifts awakened a new Spring that threw off the shackles of the Angel's Winter and the people at last grew straight and strong. The veils with which science and religion had blinded them for so long crumpled and fell away from their minds, and they saw SPACE and TIME and CONSCIOUSNESS coalesce into a solitary unified vision; and a fresh cycle of understanding finally began.

HARMONY swirled through this genesis like a thousand wheeling honey bees spiralling kaleidoscopically outward to drive all distrust from the land; and the Philosopher's WISDOM spread ever into the souls of the people, until its swelling power and glory drove the final floundering remnants of Lucifer into the chains of his thousand-year exile. The people could now turn themselves inward towards the one true goal worthy of the spirit of a man – ETERNITY. And the young boy's Seventh and Final Gift gave the inspiration and strength needed for this great journey into the farthest reaches of their souls.

The Seven Gifts - Angel

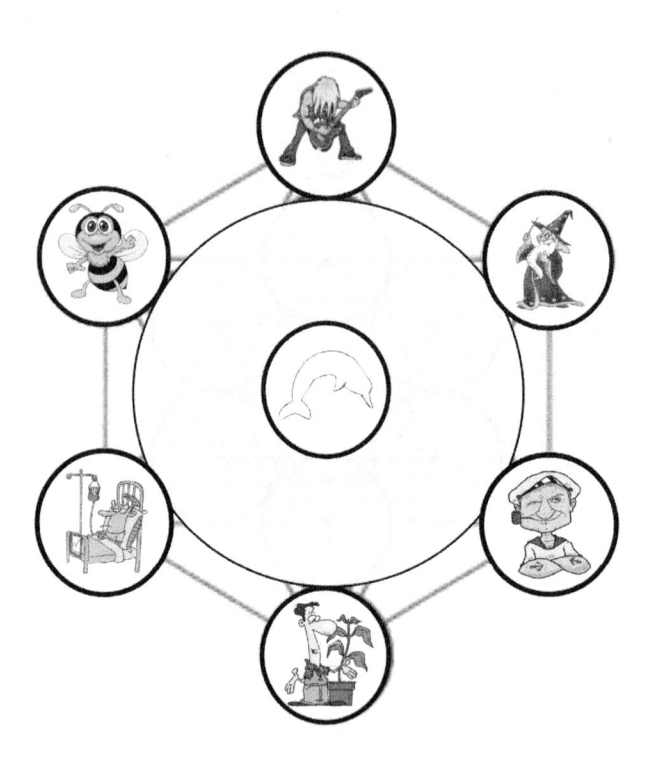

Like the white dolphin, his most precious gift of them all – LOVE – swam soundless and endless through all their hearts; guiding them ever onward, safely away from the spiritual death and darkness of their earthly materialism towards the true destiny of immortal men.

~ ~ ~ ~ ~ ~ ~

The young boy brought all this to them

with a little help from the Angel

AND as we each of us now go also
through our own endless personal cycles
of hope and disillusionment

As each one of us struggles to free his soul
from the chains of these material bonds

As each of us seeks to strengthen
his spirit for the singer

So the Angel
through the eyes of her Fairy Tern
watches us too

For this is not the end of the story
This is the beginning

The end of the story we write ourselves

with a little help from the Angel :

*Lay not up for yourselves
treasures upon earth
where moth and rust doth corrupt
and where thieves break through and steal*

*but lay up for yourselves
treasures in heaven
where neither moth nor rust doth corrupt
and thieves do not break through nor steal*

*for where your treasure is
there will your heart be also*

Then will the Fairy Tern

wheel on her long white wings

and leave

The Angel

will wipe away all the tears

from our eyes

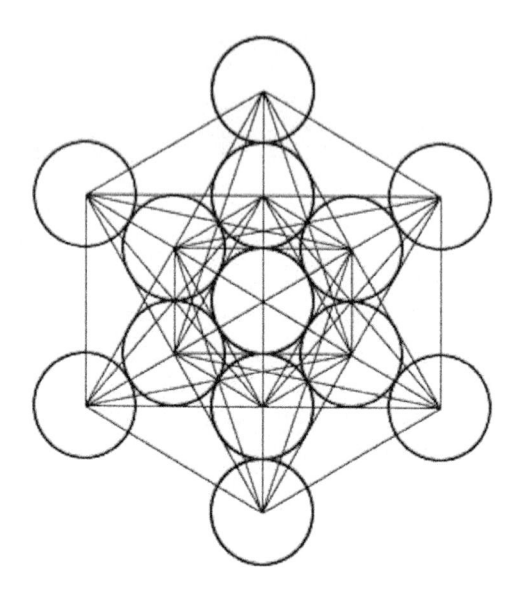

And we none of us

will ever again

be the people we were.

Be not forgetful to entertain strangers
for thereby some have met the Angel unawares

Printed by Amazon Italia Logistica S.r.l.
Torrazza Piemonte (TO), Italy